The Vanishing Of
AVELINE JONES

To Mum, who's doing her own vanishing trick.
Thank you for everything.

First published in the UK in 2022 by Usborne Publishing Limited., Usborne House,
83-85 Saffron Hill, London EC1N 8RT, England, usborne.com

Usborne Verlag, Usborne Publishing Ltd., Prüfeninger Str. 20, 93049 Regensburg,
Deutschland, VK Nr. 17560

Text copyright © Phil Hickes, 2022

The right of Phil Hickes to be identified as the author of this work has been asserted by him
in accordance with the Copyright, Designs and Patents Act, 1988.

Illustrations copyright © Usborne Publishing Limited., 2022

Illustrations by Keith Robinson.

Cover typography by Sarah J Coleman/inkymole.com

The name Usborne and the Balloon logo are Trade Marks of Usborne Publishing Limited.

A CIP catalogue record for this book is available from the British Library.

JFMAMJ ASOND/24 ISBN 9781474972161 05659/3

Printed and bound using 100% renewable electricity by CPI Group (UK) Ltd, CR0 4YY

The Vanishing Of AVELINE JONES

Phil Hickes

Illustrated by Keith Robinson

USBORNE

"Sometimes, those who are carried off
are allowed, after many years, a final glimpse
of their friends."

The Celtic Twilight,
William Butler Yeats, 1893

Chapter 1
A Mystery Awaits

Lulled by the rhythmic clickety-clack of the train, Aveline's eyelids drooped. Sleep reached out with its soft, spongy arms, but she resisted and blinked herself awake. Outside, the countryside drowned beneath a watery deluge, the rain hurling itself horizontally across the landscape like a fistful of grey nails. Grim mires of dark water pooled in the fields. Black clouds billowed like clenched fists. Frowning, Aveline pushed back her glasses. This was supposed to be the best time of the year. The laziest. The comfiest. The most magical. School had finished and the Christmas holidays had started. By now, she should have been existing mainly on chocolate, watching films in her zebra onesie, and curled up on the cushions in front of the fire reading her favourite books. Nothing to do and all day to do it. Instead, here she was, sitting on a hard seat in a chilly train carriage with a rumbling stomach.

They were on their way to a village called Scarbury, about fifty miles away from their home in Bristol. Aveline's Uncle Rowan lived there – or at least he used to live there – before he'd disappeared.

Aveline had only been two years old at the time, but her mum had told her a little bit about what had happened. It had been December, almost ten years ago. He had gone out one day, and just never came back. At first, everyone expected Uncle Rowan to reappear. It wasn't that unusual for him to go AWOL every now and then. But as time passed, and he didn't return, it quickly went from odd, to weird, to worrying. No sightings. No clues. Just thin air and an empty house gathering dust and junk mail. Since that day, Uncle Rowan had never been heard from again. And so, eventually, the time had come when her mum had to accept that, miracles aside, he wouldn't be coming back. And with mortgage payments on his house still outstanding, they would need to sell it. It was a sad task for Aveline's mum, almost like an official goodbye, which is why she'd wanted to conclude matters before Christmas.

Blinking out of her trance, Aveline glanced across the table, which was covered with coffee cups, mobile phones, biscuit wrappers, books and a scattered deck of playing cards. Opposite her, Aunt Lilian twitched in her seat. She'd fallen into a doze sometime after they boarded the train. Even in her sleep, she frowned slightly, obviously displeased at whatever was happening in her dreams. This trip would be hard on her, too. Uncle Rowan was her younger brother. Normally strong and assured about everything, right now, Aunt Lilian looked small and fragile. Aveline would have gone and sat beside her, and maybe leaned into her a little, but Aveline's mum was sleeping, too, her head lolling against Aunt Lilian's shoulder. Aveline silently promised herself that she would try to be there for them both over the next few days.

Rummaging in her backpack, Aveline retrieved the only photo she had of herself and her Uncle Rowan. She pulled it close to her face. Then she drew it away until it was in her lap, peering at it through half-closed eyes. She repeated this motion a couple of times, like a detective examining an important clue. The photograph had a white border around it, and the colours had faded. It showed a man standing by the edge of a lake, wearing hiking shorts and a grubby blue T-shirt. He had long, straight, black hair, parted in the middle, and small, round glasses with wire frames, behind which narrowed eyes peered suspiciously at the camera. By far, his most striking feature was his bushy beard, which sprawled over the lower half of his face. He was holding the hand of a tiny girl who resembled a baby bird that had fallen out of the nest. Aveline smiled at her younger self, hoping that these days she didn't look quite so scruffy and bewildered.

"Does it ring any bells?" her mum said with a tired smile.

Aveline shook her head. She hadn't realized her mum had woken up.

"No, sorry, Mum."

"Don't be sorry, love, you were only tiny. But you remember me talking about him when you got older?"

"A bit," Aveline said, wanting her mum to talk more about his disappearance but afraid to ask. Her mum always seemed reluctant to discuss *that* part of Uncle Rowan's life, and Aveline was sure there must be more to it than the few vague details she had. In the end, she settled for a safer option. "What was he like?"

Aveline's mum smiled sadly, before beginning to clear their lunch leftovers off the table.

"Very kind. Super smart. Generous to a fault. But

always very shy, even with his own family. He definitely kept his cards close to his chest."

"How do you mean?" Aveline asked. She wanted to know Uncle Rowan better; her own memories were so vague.

"Well, I'd suddenly find it was time to say goodbye to him and realize that I'd been speaking about myself the whole time. I think he liked to keep his private life... well...private. I wish I'd taken more time to be with him, but I was a busy, single mum and, sometimes, all I could think about was getting through to the end of the day in one piece. I suppose in some respects, we drifted apart. It happens – you're so absorbed in your own life and your own problems that you forget about everybody else's until it's too late."

Her mum nudged a knuckle at the corner of her eye, as if she'd drifted off into her own little world for a moment. Aveline glanced away. The rain left glistening scars on the train windows. More sodden, lifeless fields sped by, reflecting the sombre mood in the train carriage. Aveline wanted to say something upbeat, but it was hard to find the words. The bleak winter weather dampened everything, including her spirits.

"What did Uncle Rowan do, you know, as a job?"

"He was an archaeologist. It meant he worked alone, a lot, which I think suited him very well. And he always seemed to be rushing off somewhere, which is probably why we didn't get to see him that much. But even though you didn't get to know him, Aveline, I do know that he thought the world of you."

A tingle of pleasure warmed Aveline's cheeks.

"Really?"

"Oh, yes. He didn't have any children of his own, you see, so he quite took to his new niece after you were born. He called you *Little Ave*, and you were equally taken with him, following him around like a baby duck paddling after its mother."

"No, I did not!"

"I thought you said you couldn't remember anything?" Aveline's mum said with a *gotcha* grin. Glancing at her watch, Aveline's mum eased herself out of her seat. "I think we're nearly there, love. I'm just popping to the loo."

Aveline leaned back into her seat with a smile. It felt good to know that her Uncle Rowan had loved her. She only wished he hadn't vanished before she'd got the chance to get to know him better. If only she could discover what had happened. Maybe he was still out there somewhere?

"Tickets, please!"

Glancing up, Aveline saw Harold, his floppy fringe framing a giant grin. As always, she was glad he was here. Him *and* his terrible jokes. She hadn't been sure he'd want to come, but his mum and dad were away with their furniture business again, and with school having just finished for the holidays, he had a few days free and nothing better to do. Also, Aveline had told him that they were here to solve a mystery, which while more of a *hope* than a *fact*, had intrigued him enough to agree to join her.

"I'd keep my voice down if I were you," Aveline whispered. "If my aunt wakes up, she might decide you need to do some extra study."

With a nervous glance at Aunt Lilian, Harold squeezed in next to Aveline.

"You know, trying to pee on a train isn't easy," he said in a low voice.

"Thanks for the update," Aveline said, which made Harold snicker. She could happily live life without knowing the grisly details of Harold's bathroom challenges.

"So, what's the plan then?" Harold said, twirling his dark fringe around his finger like strands of liquorice.

"We're putting my Uncle Rowan's house on the market."

Harold paused, letting the strand of hair unwind itself.

"No, I mean, aren't we going to try and find out more about…" Harold gave Aunt Lilian another quick glance. "You know."

"His disappearance?" Aveline whispered.

"Yes, I mean, it's strange that we don't know much about what happened. You'd think they might have CCTV or something."

Pushing back her glasses, Aveline sighed.

"It was ten years ago, Harold, and he lives in a small village. Not sure they were hooked up with a state-of-the-art CCTV system."

"He could have been kidnapped."

"No ransom notes. Besides, I'm not sure that scruffy archaeologists without much money are high up on the list of kidnap targets."

Harold shrugged his shoulders.

"Witness protection programme? I dunno, maybe he saw something he shouldn't have and was given a new identity."

"While possible –" Aveline said, screwing up her face – "I really doubt he witnessed any mafia deals in a small village near Cheltenham."

"Alright, fair enough. Do you have any theories?"

"No, but that's exactly what we're here for," Aveline said. "And you know what's going to help us? We're going to have his house all to ourselves. Mum arranged for a cleaner to go in every now and then, but apart from that, it hasn't been touched. It should be just as he left it. There's got to be something in there that's going to tell us more."

Harold sat up in his seat, his eyes shining at the prospect.

"Okay, what's the name of the place where he lives again?"

"Scarbury."

Harold fell silent, pulled out his phone and began to look at something. After a few minutes he said *woah* under his breath and began to move his fingers really fast as though he was reading something fascinating. Eventually, Aveline couldn't help but peer over.

"What are you looking at that's so interesting?"

"Thought you would have already found this yourself."

"Found what?"

Harold raised his eyebrows. "Take a look."

Handing her his phone, Harold sat back and crossed his arms. Pushing back her glasses, Aveline saw that he'd been reading a blog.

The Spooky Blogspot

Strange Lights Spotted Above Scarbury

A number of people living in and around Scarbury have reported seeing ghostly lights at night, again, close to the old long barrow. Residents shared pictures and videos on social media, many claiming that the lights appeared to be moving. Mike Williams, 42, a local builder, said that generations of his family have witnessed the strange phenomenon. "My grandmother used to call the lights will-o'-the-wisps. She told me they were evil faeries, trying to lure unsuspecting travellers off the path, sometimes into bogs and rivers where they would drown. My father used to see the lights a lot, too, and he always told me never to follow them." However, local geologist, Mia Khan, offers an alternative explanation. "As organic matter in waterlogged fields and marshes breaks down, it releases flammable toxic gases that can often burst into flame as they come into contact with the air. I strongly suspect that this is what people are actually seeing."

Posted Dec 16, 2021 by:

Sammy-Adamu-Taylor11@SpookyBlogspot

Aveline handed him back the phone. "That's weird. How did you find it?"

"There's this thing called the internet, see, and if you type stuff into your browser it—"

Aveline pushed him away.

"You could be a comedian, Harold...if only you had some funny jokes."

They were interrupted by the sound of a crackly voice over the train tannoy.

We'll shortly be arriving at Cheltenham, where this train will terminate. Please remember to take all your belongings with you when you leave and thank you for travelling with Great Western Railway. Next stop, Cheltenham.

Blinking furiously, Aunt Lilian shot up from her seat and began to hurriedly help pack away their belongings, while Aveline's mum arrived back from the loo and started handing down their bags. As Aveline disembarked onto the windswept platform, needles of icy rain blew into her face. Shivering, she bowed her head. Now that they'd actually arrived, everything seemed slightly daunting.

Her uncle, gone.

A house, abandoned.

Answers, none.

But she was determined to find some. Her mum and aunt needed to know.

Taking a deep breath, she followed the others through the ticket gates. Thankfully, there was a row of taxis waiting outside, their exhausts sending plumes of petrol-scented smoke into the air. A man with a shaven head wound down his window when he saw them approach.

"Now then, am I right in thinking that you four will be wanting a taxi?" the taxi driver said in a cheery voice.

"You would indeed be correct," Aunt Lilian said. "These four will be very grateful if you could take them to Scarbury."

While the driver loaded their bags into the boot, they climbed in, with Aunt Lilian assuming a position of authority in the front seat. After being outside in the cold, the warm air humming through the taxi felt like a hug, and Aveline stretched out her cold toes.

After they'd navigated their way through Cheltenham's busy streets, the lanes narrowed. The houses grew older and more historic. Huge trees lined the road, their branches hanging above the pavements like leafy umbrellas. The modern street lights fell away to be replaced by the occasional lamp, and in the darkening afternoon, it did feel a little as if they'd stepped back in time. Aveline felt a flicker of apprehension as their final destination drew near. With a hiss of tyres on the damp road, the taxi drew to a halt.

Aveline peered out of the window at a large, two-storey house, built from sandstone. Iron railings fenced it off from the road. A solitary lamp post stood guard outside. Steps led up to a path and then on to a porch, above which dark windows glinted like suspicious eyes. A sign on the gate read:

Bier House.

Aveline took a deep breath.

The truth to Uncle Rowan's disappearance could lie somewhere within these four walls.

"Fairies are frequently described as being peevish, irritable, and revengeful to a degree."

British Fairy Origins,
Lewis Spence, 1946

Chapter 2
The Midnight Visitor

Fishing a key out of her purse, Aunt Lilian led them through the gate. As she unlocked the front door, a chill draught rushed out like a fleeing ghost. The door only opened a fraction, a mountain of junk mail piled stubbornly behind it, but with a well-aimed kick from her pointy shoes, Aunt Lilian sent it flying, and they entered.

In front of them, a staircase led up into a discomfiting darkness. Aunt Lilian flicked the light on, and the hallway lit up with a sickly yellow glow. A grandfather clock stood silently in the gloom. The hallway table had a phone on it and behind it, a long mirror with an ornate wooden frame stretched almost from the ceiling to the floor. Most houses had a lived-in feel, Aveline thought. You'd smell what everyone had eaten for breakfast. There'd be dirty shoes by the door. A cat might be sat in a window swishing its tail, or a dog would come and give you a welcome wag. This house had an unnerving emptiness about it. A stale smell. Even if you knew nothing about the house and its sad history, you could still sense that it hadn't been occupied for some time.

At the end of the hallway, Aveline could see strange shadows leaping around the walls as her aunt explored the kitchen.

"The good news is that the heating appears to be working," she called out.

"Well, at least we'll be warm," Aveline's mum said, seeming a little apprehensive herself.

"That's the spirit, Susan," Aunt Lilian called back. "Come and give me a hand, will you? I need a volunteer for potato-peeling duties."

Aveline's mum rolled her eyes.

"I can't believe she brought a bag of groceries with her on the train," she whispered. "Hasn't she ever heard of takeaways?"

Aveline watched her mum go. She seemed stressed, which was understandable, given the circumstances. She was glad to hear the heating was working, though, because it was uncomfortably cold. Aveline's breaths came out in ghostly clouds. In the darkness of the hallway, Harold looked like a shadow.

There were two closed doors in the hallway, one on their right and one on their left. Harold motioned to them.

"Left or right?"

"Right," Aveline said, turning the knob on the door. Were the first clues about to be revealed? It opened with a creak, revealing a sparsely furnished room. Just a coffee table and two uncomfortable-looking wooden chairs. Nothing on the walls, bare floorboards. There was a fireplace, its blackened grate telling them that it must have been used once, but probably a long time ago. It smelled of dust and furniture polish, the latter probably thanks to the cleaners that still came in occasionally.

"Oh," Harold said, failing to hide his disappointment. Aveline was disappointed, too. She'd told Harold the house had lain untouched, which had got them both excited, but this wasn't how she imagined it to be. Maybe the house had been cleaned out after all?

"Let's try the other one," Aveline said.

Harold stepped across the hallway and twisted the knob. "Locked."

"Really?"

"Either that or it's protected by an invisible force field."

Aveline wrinkled her nose. "Hmm, I wonder what's inside? There must be a key somewhere." Impatiently, she looked around and spotted a small wooden door underneath the staircase. "Maybe in there?"

She walked over and opened it, then fumbled around in the dark for a light switch. A cord hung from the ceiling. She gave it a yank and up above, a bare light bulb flickered into life. Hanging from hooks, there were old waterproofs that smelled of mould. On a narrow shelf there was a torch, which Aveline grabbed and switched on to give them a little more light. In one corner, she could see a pile of old junk mail, probably dumped there by the cleaners. Next to these envelopes full of offers for credit cards, car insurance and home loans, there was a stack of newspapers. Harold wedged himself in beside her.

"Can't see any keys, can you?"

"Nope."

"Maybe we could pick the lock or something, I mean, we've got to get in there somehow and…"

He trailed off as Aveline's mum came to join them.

"What are you two doing hanging about in the cupboard like a couple of coats in search of a hook? Come and have something to eat; there'll be plenty of time later to have a nose around."

In the kitchen, Aunt Lilian stood at the stove, harassing some sausages around a sizzling skillet. A pan full of boiling water bubbled beside it, loaded to the brim with potatoes. Unlike everything else they'd seen so far, the kitchen retained some sense of Uncle Rowan's character. Blackened saucepans hung from hooks. There was a large wooden dining table. Pictures hung on the wall. One photograph showed him as a young man, standing in a trench with a muddy trowel in one hand, holding up what might have been an earthenware pot in the other. A big grin on his face suggested he was pretty pleased to have found it. There were colourful magnets on the fridge freezer door. Aveline glanced at one.

Archaeologist. (Noun.)

One crackpot digging up another cracked pot.

Smirking to herself, she opened the back door and beckoned to Harold. Walking out, they found themselves in a conservatory. Aveline glanced up at the glass ceiling, seeing a reflection of a girl with wonky glasses and a boy with messy hair peering back, like two ghostly versions of themselves that just happened to live on the roof. At the back door lay a pair of weathered boots and a walking stick, together with a couple of jackets on hooks. Picking up the boots, Aveline inspected them. They were quite worn out, to the point that one even had a small hole in the sole. Narrowing her eyes, Aveline put them back where she found them. Obviously her uncle had been outdoors a lot, which she sort of knew already. These things told her little snippets about her uncle's day-to-day life. They told her absolutely nothing about his disappearance. It wasn't the start she'd hoped for.

"Mum, one of the doors in the hallway is locked. Do you have a key?"

Aveline knew that if there were any answers to be found, this room was currently the most promising lead.

Pausing with a potato masher in her hand, Aveline's mum frowned.

"You know, the cleaners asked me that, too, but I'm not sure where Rowan keeps it."

"It's Rowan's study, if I remember rightly," Aunt Lilian said. "He always locked it when he went out. When he went missing, the police unlocked it, just in case he was in there, but I have no idea what they did with the key. Probably lost it, I expect. Anyway, I can put a locksmith on my to-do list since Susan obviously forgot to put it on hers."

"So glad you're here to point out my mistakes," Aveline's mum said.

"My pleasure," Aunt Lilian snapped back.

Aveline grimaced at Harold, who made an *uh-oh* face. Yet, once the meal was ready, things seemed to calm down. The sausages and mash gave them all the pleasant feeling of a full belly, and Aveline's mum and aunt seemed to relax a little more into each other's company, much to Aveline's relief. At the same time, the heating kicked in, and the house began to feel more welcoming.

"Well, I suppose we best get the bedrooms sorted," Aveline's mum said. "You two can come and give me a hand."

As Harold followed her mum upstairs, Aveline hung back and tried the locked door again, giving it a hard wiggle as if that might do the trick, but whatever secrets lay behind it refused to reveal themselves. Getting on all fours, Aveline peered beneath the crack in the doorway. A street light shone through the windows, but she couldn't see much. The legs of a chair. Some papers. The bottom of a desk, perhaps. But it smelled different to the other room; of dust and wood and leather.

Then, for a second, a shadow passed across the light.

Aveline flung herself back in shock. Her glasses slipped

and fell across the bridge of her nose. Her heart accelerated to 100mph. She forced herself to breathe. Probably just someone walking down the street outside, their shadow cast into the room as they passed.

"Are you okay?" Aunt Lilian emerged from the kitchen, wiping her hands on a tea towel. "I heard an almighty thump. What's the matter? Did you slip? Are you hurt?"

"N-no...I..." Aveline fought to get some breath back into her body. "I was just looking under the door and made myself jump."

"Silly you then," Aunt Lilian said without any humour in her voice. "This is a large and gloomy house, so please let's not start making it feel more unsettling than it already is."

And with that, Aunt Lilian marched back into the kitchen. Aveline felt annoyed for a second. It wasn't her fault that she'd startled herself. But then she tried to imagine how Aunt Lilian must be feeling. Walking into the kitchen, where her aunt had returned to drying the dishes, Aveline reached up from behind and gave her aunt a hug.

"I'm sorry I snapped at you, Aveline," Aunt Lilian said, reaching down to squeeze Aveline's hands. "It's just... it makes me so sad seeing Rowan's house without Rowan in it."

"I know."

"Go on then, best get yourself upstairs. Harold's probably bagged the best bedroom."

On her way to join the others upstairs and foil Harold's best-laid plans, Aveline paused to peer into the long hallway mirror. In the gloom, the dust on the surface made her reflection look old and faded, as if she were looking at an antique version of herself. Like a Victorian doll, perched on a bed in some old house, staring sightlessly out at the world. It gave her the creeps, so she quickly scuttled upstairs, the middle stair groaning as if it resented being stepped on.

Harold and her mum were busily piling quilts, pillows and blankets on the beds. The bedrooms had yet to feel the benefits of the central heating and the harsh clacking of cold rain on the windows made Aveline want to immediately jump beneath the sheets. Nobody wanted to sleep in Uncle Rowan's empty bedroom, so it had been decided that she and Harold would sleep in adjoining rooms. An inside door connected the two rooms together. While Aunt Lilian and her mum made their own rooms comfortable, Aveline and Harold chatted before going to bed. With his toothbrush stuck in one cheek, like a hamster storing a nut, and dressed in a bizarre combination of pyjamas, striped socks pulled to his knees, and an oversized dressing gown that he'd found in one of the cupboards, Harold seemed well prepared for the cold night ahead. Aveline told him what she'd seen downstairs.

"What do you think it was?" he said.

"Oh, I don't know, probably someone walking down the street."

"Must have given you a fright though, eh?"

"Yes, my glasses fell off and Aunt Lilian got angry with me. But seriously, Harold, we have to find a key for that study. Why else would it be locked unless there's something important in there?"

Smiling, Harold took out his toothbrush. "Okay, well, that's our priority for tomorrow. And locksmith or not, we won't stop until we find a way in, alright? Anyway, I'm off to bed; it's freezing in here. If anything happens in the night, knock once, then twice, then I'll know it's you."

Aveline laughed.

"Who else do you think it's going to be?"

"Dunno, ghost or something? See you in the morning."

"Night."

As she snuggled into her bedclothes, it took a while, but Aveline finally began to feel properly warm, probably for the first time that day. She put thoughts of the study and locked doors and creeping shadows out of her mind. Just as she began to feel as though she was sinking into a giant pile of feathers, and her mind began to wander into the misty world of dreams...

A long, slow creak.

Creeee-ak.

Aveline opened her eyes.

It was as if a foot had pressed down hard on one of the stairs.

The house lay silent, holding its breath, waiting to see what she would do.

Aveline strained to listen, dreading the sound of footsteps. When none came, she slowly inched her feet out of bed and searched in the dark for her slippers. Sliding them on, she pulled her dressing gown from the top of the bedclothes, grabbed the torch she'd found earlier, and crept to the door.

Opening it a crack, she shined a light out onto the landing.

"Harold?" she whispered, thinking that he might have been going downstairs to use the loo or something. But the silence was so thick, she knew immediately that it wasn't him.

"Hello?" she called again.

Peering down the stairs, for a moment she thought she saw something – or someone – about halfway down. Fear clawed at her limbs with icy nails. It looked like a small, hunched figure, scrabbling and scratching at the steps like a dog burying a bone.

With shaky hands, Aveline slowly raised her torch, the beam creeping down the stairs one by one until...

Light flooded onto the landing. Turning, Aveline saw her mum step out of her bedroom. She flashed her torch back down the stairs, but all she could see now was an empty staircase leading down to the silent hallway.

"I might have known, the midnight wanderer strikes again," her mum said. "Are you okay, Aveline, did you need something?"

"It's nothing," Aveline said, suppressing a shudder. "Just thought I heard somebody on the stairs."

Walking to the top of the stairs, her mum peered down.

"The only thing I can see is an old musty carpet that probably needs chucking out as soon as possible. So, if you're in agreement, let's get back to bed; it's freezing out here."

Aveline didn't reply. She hurried back to bed, where warm sheets were waiting to comfort her. Burrowing her face in the pillows, she tried to forget what she'd seen.

Or thought she'd seen.

It was no good. Her mind was racing, and she needed to speak to someone about it.

And by *someone*, she meant Harold.

"Sometimes one may thus go to Faerie for an hour or two; or one may remain there for seven, fourteen, or twenty-one years."

The Fairy-Faith in Celtic Countries,
Walter Evans-Wentz, 1911

Chapter 3
Secrets Unlocked

Aveline knocked on Harold's door. Real or not, she couldn't stop thinking about the figure on the stairs, and she didn't want to be alone right now. There was silence for a moment before Harold called out in a muffled voice.

"What's the code?"

Sighing, Aveline knocked twice more.

"Seriously, Harold?" she said as he opened the door and waved her in, scratching at his messy bed hair.

"Better safe than sorry," he said in all seriousness. "Why are you up in the middle of the night?"

"Well...I'm not exactly sure but..." Aveline trailed off.

Harold's eyes widened. He wrapped his arms around

himself and rubbed the top of his shoulders.

"Oh no. What did you see? It was a ghost, wasn't it? You have to tell me, Aveline, it wasn't the ghost of your—"

"No, it wasn't Uncle Rowan, Harold. But I did think I saw something on the stairs. I heard a creak, just after we went to bed."

"What was it?"

"I don't know, couldn't see it properly, but it looked like a person. Sort of crouched over, as if they were looking for something. It was pitch black though."

"Really? Show me."

"Okay, but we have to be quiet. I've already woken my mum up once."

Together, they sneaked out of Harold's bedroom and crept down the stairs until around halfway down.

"Here, I think," Aveline whispered, beginning to regret not going straight back to bed.

Harold stepped down to the next stair, then up again, pressing down with both feet. The stair let out a loud creak.

"Shush!" Aveline hissed.

Harold held up his hands in a silent apology.

"Is that the right place?"

Aveline nodded.

"I think so."

Bending down, they had a look. Harold ran his hands over the carpet, frowning as his fingers ran over a noticeable bump.

"There's something underneath here," he whispered.

Looking at Aveline, he pointed down. They felt around at the edges of the stair. It was difficult to see in the gloom, but Aveline was able to work her fingers underneath the carpet. As she pulled it back, it came away easily as if it had never been nailed down or glued. Underneath was a key. Aveline shivered as if a cold breeze had just blown in from outside.

"I reckon I can guess which keyhole that might fit into," Harold whispered, swatting away his fringe like a bothersome fly.

Aveline glanced downstairs. It was so quiet and dark. She could easily imagine someone waiting down there, just out of sight. But Harold was right. This had to be it, the missing key they'd been desperate to find. Grabbing it, they crept down the stairs trying to make as little noise as possible. Aveline's hands shook with a mixture of excitement and fear. It took her a few seconds to slide the key into the study door. Taking a deep breath, she turned it. It stuck. She wiggled it around and tried again. Then they heard a neat click and the door swung open.

"Finally!" Harold said, reaching in a hand. Flicking the light switch, they heard a strange hum, as if the bulb had just been shaken awake after a long sleep.

Then they stepped in.

It had to be one of the most bizarre rooms Aveline had ever been in. Part explorer's camp, part laboratory, part wizard's cave, part cosy nook, part artist's studio, every single surface – including parts of the ceiling – had been covered with pictures, sketches, charts, diagrams, maps, Post-it notes, newspaper cuttings, pages torn from books and various artwork. There was a huge mahogany desk, a chair, a brass lamp, a battered old leather sofa, a woodstove, a giant wardrobe and a crammed bookcase that had long since reached breaking point; books spilled out over the floor like groceries from burst supermarket bags. There were strangely shaped glass bottles and vials on one shelf. A pendulum hanging from a nail. Strange figurines that appeared to be half human and half animal. Scented candles. A pack of tarot cards. A crystal ball. In one corner, there was even a camp bed, suggesting that this was a room that Uncle Rowan rarely left. It felt woody and warm, with a russet rug stretched out in front of the woodstove like a cat.

"This is more like it," Harold said.

"Wow," Aveline said, wondering where to start. It was a jigsaw puzzle without a guide to follow, but there had to be *something* in here that would tell her more about her Uncle Rowan and his life.

Aveline went to the wardrobe. There was a mirror on the front with a sticker that said:

An Archaeologist's career lies in ruins.

"These archaeology jokes are almost as bad as yours, Harold," Aveline said, pulling the wardrobe open. Inside there were wax jackets hanging from hooks but not much else.

Harold plonked himself down in front of the bookcase and began pulling out the books, frowning at each one, before placing them to one side and grabbing another.

"Your uncle's got similar reading tastes to you by the looks of it," Harold called out.

"Keep it down, Harold!" Aveline hissed.

"Sorry," Harold said, quieter this time. "But you've got to see these."

He held up a few books for Aveline to look at.

The Underworld and its Citizens.
Contacting the Dead.
The Power of Crystals.
Ley Lines & The Mystical Network.
Astrology in the Landscape.

"Wow," Aveline said again, feeling a sudden closeness to her uncle that she'd never really experienced before. "I had no idea. I just thought he was into history."

"Doesn't look like it. Those are just the tip of the iceberg, too; there are loads of them here."

Aveline took another look around the room, taking in details she hadn't noticed at first glance. A frightening-looking mask gazed sightlessly at her from the wall.

A poster advertised a *Psychic Festival* in somewhere called Harrogate. There was an otherworldly feel to it all. She turned to what appeared to be her uncle's noticeboard, though its contents had broken free of the frame and spread out to the rest of the wall. The first thing that caught her attention was a newspaper cutting.

A CHRISTMAS DISAPPEARANCE, STILL UNSOLVED AFTER SEVENTY YEARS.

WHAT HAPPENED TO THE SCARBURY SCHOOLGIRLS?

"Harold, look," Aveline said. "Missing people. In Scarbury. My uncle kept the newspaper report and put it on the wall – why would he do that?"

Harold glanced up with a puzzled frown.

"What's it say?"

Aveline did her best to give Harold the essential information. It concerned two schoolgirls, Mary and Fiona, who had gone missing in Scarbury many years ago just before Christmas, while on a school history trip to a long barrow. The case had never been solved. It had been a puzzling incident and the journalist had decided to write

45

about it in the hope that someone might still come forward with information. Uncle Rowan didn't have anything else on the wall that suggested they'd come any closer to solving what happened.

"Why do you think your uncle would be interested in that?" Harold said. "Was he an amateur detective as well as an archaeologist?"

"I don't know, maybe? But there's another article here, right next to it."

It was a photocopy of a newspaper article from the 1970s. This time Harold came and read it himself.

WORKMAN PRESUMED DROWNED.
December 27, 1973.

The search for a missing employee of Cheltenham Water Company was officially called off today. Bob Andrews, 43, had been working in Scarbury on a drainage project in and around the area close to the long barrow. It is believed he may have been caught up in a flash flood after heavy rainfall swelled the local river to record levels, but until his body is located, police are refusing to speculate. The man's family are being kept up to date with developments.

"So," Harold said, scratching his hair, which was still

sticking up from when he'd been asleep. "Your uncle was interested in people that were missing in the area – and now he's missing, too. Seems a bit of a coincidence, doesn't it?"

"Yes, it does," Aveline said. "And you know what's really weird? Both articles mention the long barrow, same as that blog post you showed me. I wonder where exactly it is?"

"Maybe we can find it on here," Harold said, pointing to a large map that had been pinned to the wall.

They spent a few minutes examining it before Aveline suddenly spotted what they'd been looking for and pressed a finger to the map.

"There!"

A symbol like a postage stamp, beneath which was written:

Scarbury Long Barrow.

Historical Landmark.

"This is your uncle's house here," Harold said, pressing his finger up beside Aveline's. "So the barrow looks like it's just...half a finger away!"

"That's helpful, Harold," Aveline laughed, before looking at the scale at the bottom of the map. Placing her finger alongside it, she worked out that it was roughly half a mile or so away.

"Walking distance," she said. "We have to go and see it."

"Look, there's a photo of it here," Harold said.

Aveline examined it. It was black and white and showed a group of men standing by a hill, though it was no ordinary hill, more of a long and unnaturally shaped mound. Aveline thought it looked like a submarine made of grass and there were huge stone slabs at one end. The men all had moustaches and wore flat caps, and in their hands they held shovels and pickaxes. They all looked very serious, except for a figure standing in shadow behind the group, right on top of the curious mound. Aveline couldn't be sure, the photograph was very old, but it looked like they might have been smiling. The caption said *Scarbury Long Barrow Excavation, 1904*. Every inch of Uncle Rowan's study was proving to be both useful and mystifying.

"Harold," Aveline asked, trailing a finger over the photograph; "what is a *long barrow* exactly?"

Harold flicked his fringe.

"Well, you know, like a wheelbarrow? A long barrow is the same except that it's really, really long."

"You don't know, do you?" Aveline said, trying not to

give Harold the satisfaction of seeing her grin.

"Nope."

Aveline pulled out her phone and typed *Scarbury Long Barrow* into the search bar. The result flicked up.

Scarbury Long Barrow is a prehistoric monument in the south-west of England that dates to the Early Neolithic period. Similar examples can be found across Western Europe. Archaeological excavations have uncovered a wide range of human remains at these sites, suggesting they were used as either community or high-prestige burial chambers. The Scarbury Long Barrow is noted for its alignment with the winter solstice sunrise, during which its passage and chamber are illuminated.

She read it out to Harold.

"So…it's like a fancy grave for cavemen?" he said.

"I suppose, something like that," Aveline said.

Turning her attention back to the desk, she began riffling through a stack of cardboard folders. One held a bundle of receipts. There were bank statements and bills. Correspondence from an accountant. Nothing out of the ordinary. All pretty boring, everyday stuff. Then there were more folders, more bills, and things that might have been important ten years ago but had long since ceased to matter.

Then, in a bottom drawer, Aveline found something way more interesting. She knew what they were because her mum still used them: a small pile of old cassette tapes. Intrigued, she picked one up. On it, written in biro, was a short note.

Session One. September 22nd

The others were all labelled similarly.

Session Two. October 31st
Session Three. December 21st
Session Four. May 1st

Aveline pulled out the other drawers, rooting through them until she found what she was looking for: a cassette player to listen to the tapes on.

"Harold, here, I've found something."

Harold glanced at the cassette player and wrinkled his nose as if he'd just smelled something unpleasant.

"An antique? Nice."

"No, well, yes, but my uncle's left some cassette tapes in his desk. We can listen to them on this."

"Are you sure? Might be private."

"That hasn't stopped us before, has it? Anyway, this is important – might tell us more about why he went missing."

Aveline plugged it into the wall, before popping open the player and inserting the cassette labelled *Session One*.

"Ready?" she asked Harold. She felt like she'd just arrived at the top of a roller coaster, about to take the stomach-churning plunge down.

"Okay."

Harold came and sat on the carpet beside her, drawing his knees into his chest and hugging them. Making sure the volume was turned down low, Aveline took a deep breath, then pressed *PLAY*.

At first, all they could hear was a hissing sound. Then they heard what sounded like an object being placed on a hard surface. Following that, they heard what must have been the sound of a match being struck, followed by a faint sizzle – presumably a candle being lit. And then silence again, for a minute or so, before, finally, a voice. It was high-pitched and shaky, with a tinge of a south-west accent.

Uncle Rowan.

But it wasn't just hearing her uncle's voice after so many years that made Aveline shiver.

It was what he said.

I'm speaking to the spirits of those who have gone before. Is there anybody there…?

"At Bealltainn, or May Day, every effort was made to scare away the fairies, who were particularly dreaded at this season."

British Fairy Origins,
Lewis Spence, 1946

Chapter 4
The Séance Tapes

Aveline gasped. She reached out and grabbed Harold's arm. He held a finger to his lips as Uncle Rowan's voice came again.

Is anybody there?

Silence for a few more seconds. Outside, the wind gusted, pressing against the windows. Somewhere in the distance, an empty can rattled along the road. Part of Aveline wanted to reach out and turn off the tape, but she knew they had to keep listening.

Come into the circle. Know that this is a safe place and that you will be listened to.

"He's doing a blinkin' séance!" Harold hissed. "You know, trying to talk to the spirits of the dead!"

"Sssh!" Aveline hissed back. "I know what a séance is."

Tonight is the autumn equinox. The earth is in balance between light and dark. It is a time to speak freely. I am going to ask questions. Make the pendulum move, if you can. Swing it sideways for NO. Back and forth for YES. So, I ask again, is anybody there?

More silence. A heavy sigh.

Is anybody there? Come into the circle and speak to me if you can.

More silence. The tape hissed. The scrape of what might have been a chair being pushed back. Then a cough, followed by rustling sounds, then the recording ended.

For a while, Aveline and Harold could only stare at each other with wide eyes.

"That's...super creepy," Harold said, eventually.

"Didn't sound like it worked," Aveline said.

"Let's see if he had any success in his next session then."

Finding the appropriate cassette, Aveline inserted it.

Again, the sounds of someone getting organized. The rasp of the match. Bumps and scrapes. A nervous cough. And then after a few moments, Uncle Rowan's tremulous voice.

Halloween. Also known as Samhain in the old language.

As the sun sinks, the veil grows thinner and I invite you, spirits, to come into the circle and warm yourselves. I wish to speak in particular to Mary and Fiona. To those who were lost. Come and share your story.

Aveline dared not breathe, almost as if she was sitting in the dark herself, by the light of a solitary candle, one finger stretched out to gently touch the top of an upturned glass. She'd seen pictures of séances in books. She knew how it was done.

Uncle Rowan only said one more thing before the tape shut off.

Who took you? What happened? Was it…them?

Aveline pulled out the tape. Harold rearranged his fringe with one shaky hand.

"Mary and Fiona," Harold said with a frown.

It only took Aveline a moment to remember where she'd just seen the names.

"The two girls who went missing! My uncle's trying to find out what happened. It has to be!"

"Certainly sounds like it," Harold said. "And who's the *them* that he mentions?"

"I don't know. But he seems to be doing séances on special days of the year," Aveline said, collecting up the other tapes to look at them. "He said the first one was on the autumn equinox. The next one was Halloween of course. Then December 21st, the midwinter solstice. The last one is on May 1st. What's special about that? They call it May Day, but I'm not sure why it's special."

"Give me a minute," Harold said, getting to his feet. "Let's see if the good old internet has the answer."

With his face lit by the glow from his phone, which made him look a little bit spooky in the dark study, Harold tapped and swiped. Pausing, he stabbed his finger down on the screen and read out loud. "May 1st. Also called Beltane. The old pagan new year."

"Okay, so we have Beltane, the autumn equinox, Halloween and the midwinter solstice. Special days in the old calendar. He must have thought it would help him in some way. Maybe it's easier to contact the dead on those days?"

Harold glanced at his phone.

"Oh no."

"What is it?" Aveline asked.

Harold screwed up his face.

"My phone says it's almost 2 a.m. now which means today is December 20th. So tomorrow is the 21st," Harold pointed out. "It's one of those special days – the solstice!"

"My uncle went missing near Christmas, maybe it was actually on the solstice, too?"

"Well, shouldn't we find out if he…you know, got through to anyone?" Harold suggested, pointing at the remaining two tapes. "And if there's any more mention of…*them*?"

Nodding, Aveline played the tapes. But while it appeared that Uncle Rowan had continued trying, he'd had no success. All they could hear was him talking away to thin air, with not so much as a rattle or a knock in response.

"Hmm," Aveline said, looking around the study. "So, we've got a lot more to go on than when we arrived. Long barrows. Séances. Missing people. Special days. And goodness knows what else there is in here. I think we're getting somewhere, don't you?"

"I think so, maybe?" Harold said with a shrug. "Not quite sure how it all fits together yet, though."

"No, nor me. We just have to keep looking."

After the excitement of finding the tapes, Aveline's heart took a while to stop thudding. She knew what séances were but had never actually *heard* one for real. And while, as Harold had correctly said, it was pretty creepy, particularly the mention of *them*, Aveline also found it very sad. Her uncle had been alone here in the house, surrounded by his pendulums and incense and candles, talking away to himself without, it seemed, anything to indicate that he'd had any kind of success.

Leaning back in her Uncle Rowan's chair, she took a moment to gather her thoughts. Her eyes strayed first to the old picture of the excavation, then back to the map.

"Harold, I think we should go and pay this long barrow a visit as soon as possible."

Before Harold had a chance to answer, another voice made them both jump.

"Good grief, what on earth are you two doing?"

Aveline's mum leaned against the doorway in her dressing gown.

"We…um…found the key to Uncle Rowan's study," Aveline said. "And we…um…wanted to see what was in here."

"Well, of course, you had to do it right away and couldn't wait a few hours until morning," Aveline's mum snapped. Shaking her head, she looked around the room, her voice softening. "You know, this is just like Rowan's bedroom used to be when he was young, like a bomb had just gone off. So, where was the key?"

"Under the carpet on the stairs."

"Oh, of course." Her mum rolled her eyes. "Typical of your uncle to leave it in such an odd place. So, have you found anything interesting?"

Aveline paused, noticing Harold had glanced in her direction. He wasn't going to say anything about the séance tapes, and Aveline decided on the spur of the moment not to mention them either. It had made her sad, so what would it do to her mum and aunt? She didn't want them to think Uncle Rowan had been sitting here alone, trying to contact the dead.

"Nothing really, except that he was interested in the local long barrow," Aveline said. "We were planning on going to take a look after breakfast."

"Well, breakfast usually happens after people have slept and woken up in their beds in the morning." Aveline's mum smiled. "So come on, you can nose through the rest of this tomorrow. Time to get some sleep."

Despite being exhausted by the time she went to bed, Aveline found sleep difficult to come by. Her uncle's tapes, the sense that he was desperately searching for answers, just like her – it was hard to take it all in. Yet, eventually, she'd drifted off and woke later than usual to the delicious smell of toast, which made her stomach rumble. After breakfast, Aveline's mum and aunt announced that they were going into Scarbury to see an estate agent about the house.

"I'm not sure how long this is going to take," Aunt Lilian said. "But hopefully we'll be back by mid-afternoon."

"Can we go to see the long barrow while you're out?" Aveline asked. "We looked on the map, and it's not far away. We can walk there."

"An educational field trip," Aunt Lilian said with a triumphant smile. "How wonderful that you and Harold have chosen to broaden your minds while you're here. And I didn't even have to threaten anybody. What do you think, Susan?"

"Fine with me," Aveline's mum said. "As long as you take your phones. I've left you some sandwiches in the fridge for when you get hungry. Call if you need anything. Take your coats and scarves, it's chilly out. There's a key to the front door on the hallway table, don't lose it. And—"

"I think we've got it," Aveline said. "Stop worrying, Mum. We're only going to be tramping about in muddy fields looking for something that looks like a Neolithic burial chamber."

"Okay, well, try not to get dirty and—"

"Susan, they'll be just fine," Aunt Lilian said.

Aveline and Harold finished off their breakfast and got their coats on. Just as they were about to leave for the barrow, Aveline had a thought.

"Harold, remember that blog post you showed me on the train up here?"

Tapping his phone a couple of times, Harold held it up for her to see. *The Spooky Blogspot.*

"That's the one. Read me that email address at the bottom, would you? I can't find anything else online about the Scarbury Long Barrow. Maybe whoever wrote this knows something?"

Aveline typed it into her phone and wrote a quick message.

To: Sammy-Adamu-Taylor11@SpookyBlogspot.com
Subject: Long Barrow

Hello,
I've been reading your blog and just wondered if you knew anything more about the Scarbury Long Barrow?
Thanks,
Aveline

A few moments later, Aveline heard her phone ping. Someone had replied.

Aveline,
Don't go to the barrow alone.
Meet me at the coffee shop in Scarbury,
and I can tell you more.
It's called Barista. I'll be there in 30 mins.
Text me when you arrive. My number is…
Sammy.

Aveline read it to Harold. "He must live here. We have to go and meet him. He says we shouldn't go there on our own."

"But we don't know who he is," Harold protested, screwing up his face. "Not sure I fancy meeting a total stranger. You know the rules."

Suddenly, Aunt Lilian reappeared from the kitchen. "You most certainly do know the rules, Aveline. This boy from the internet could be anyone. I know that as a rule you like to throw caution to the wind, but I think on this occasion, it's best if I accompany you."

Aveline paused. She suspected that Aunt Lilian really just wanted to spend her morning at a coffee shop rather than an estate agent, but she knew it was probably the sensible thing to do.

"Okay," she said. Quickly, she typed back to Sammy.

Okay, thank you. We're on our way,
see you there.

Checking where *Barista* was on their phones, and after explaining the situation to Aveline's mum, the three of them were out of the door just a few moments later.

Reaching the gate, they turned and headed down into Scarbury, following the directions on Aveline's phone. Their feet squelched on the sodden leaves, autumn's soggy leftovers. The wind gusted through the spiny trees; the bare, spiky branches waving at them like witchy fingers.

But although the clouds were dark and grey, it didn't rain and all they had to contend with was a cold, insistent wind. After about only ten minutes or so, they reached the centre of Scarbury, which was just a short row of shops. They saw the coffee shop immediately, its name painted on the steamy windows.

"Well how do we find this spooky Sammy?" Aunt Lilian asked.

Frowning, Aveline tried to see through the glass.

"I said I'd text him when we got here. Let's go in. We can have a hot chocolate and a cookie while we wait."

That was enough to convince Harold and Aunt Lilian, and after ordering they found a seat by the window. It was busy, the hum of conversation loud enough to make them feel relaxed. While they were waiting for their drinks to arrive they had a look around, but with no idea what Sammy looked like, or even how old he was, it was impossible to spot any likely suspects. Aveline decided to send Sammy a text, as they'd agreed.

Hello, it's Aveline. We're in Barista. Sat by the window.

Immediately, they heard a ping from the table behind them. They turned to see a boy in a blue raincoat staring down at his phone, before he glanced up at them with a frown.

"Aveline?"

"Um, yes, hello," Aveline said, feeling herself blush. "This is my friend, Harold. And my aunt Lilian. You must be Sammy?"

"Yes. Sammy, the Spooky Blogspot."

He announced it as if *The Spooky Blogspot* was his surname. Drawing back his hood, he picked up his drink and came and sat beside them. He was around their age, Aveline guessed. His hair was black, shaved at the sides and curly on top. He wore glasses with thick, round blue frames, which had the effect of making his large, watchful eyes appear almost owl-like.

Before Aveline and Harold could say anything, Aunt Lilian burst in. "So, Sammy of the Spooky Blogspot, I assume you live in Scarbury? Do you like it here?"

"It's not bad," Sammy said without adding any further detail.

"Have you always lived here?" Aunt Lilian pressed.

"No. In London before that. My dad's parents moved back to Nigeria, so we came here to be closer to my mum's parents."

"And how old are you?"

"Eleven," Sammy said, looking a bit flustered. Aveline wondered if she needed to step in, in case Aunt Lilian planned on interrogating him all day. Besides, she wanted to ask Sammy some questions herself.

Luckily, Aunt Lilian seemed satisfied.

"Well, I'm going to take my cappuccino over by the

fire," she said. "Where I can read uninterrupted by any talk of long barrows. Lovely to meet you, Sammy."

Sammy nodded curtly and turned his attention back to his drink.

As she left, there was silence for a few moments, which began to become uncomfortable, so Aveline spoke. She suspected Sammy was probably as shy as they were.

"Sorry about my aunt, she's just making sure we're safe."

"No problem," Sammy muttered.

"Cool blog."

"Thanks."

"So…um…you know a bit about the long barrow?"

"Yes, enough to know it's dangerous," Sammy said very matter-of-factly.

"Dangerous?" Aveline said. Sammy's blunt statement took her aback. She took a sip of her drink. "Why's that?"

"Faeries live there." Seeing Harold smirk, he added, "Not the sort you're probably thinking of. I don't mean Tinkerbell and little people with wings. These are proper faeries. Also known as The Family. The Hidden People. The Fey. They're like evil spirits. And they don't like humans creeping around."

"Oh, I see," Harold said. Aveline could tell he didn't have a clue what Sammy was talking about.

Seeing Harold's face, Sammy pulled out his phone.

"Maybe it's best if I give you an example." Sammy typed something in. Then he held it out for Aveline to take. "I found this old story and put it up on my blog. You should read it. Both of you. Before we go up there. It'll help explain what we're dealing with."

Aveline took the phone and began reading.

By the time she'd finished, she felt a chill in her bones that had nothing to do with the weather.

"After you are naught but dust
and bones, we shall remain."

The Faery Mound of Scarbury,
local legend

Chapter 5
A Friendly Warning

*I*n the year 1852, a farmer bought a piece of land outside the village of Scarbury. Local people welcomed him to the community and wished him well, but as a friendly word of advice, they cautioned him never to go near the long barrow at night, because it was a faery mound, an ancient place said to be haunted by evil faeries who didn't take kindly to being disturbed. The farmer merely smiled, thanked them, and resolved in his mind to go wheresoever he wished at whatever time of day he desired. He'd paid good money for the land and didn't appreciate being instructed on how to conduct his business simply because of a silly superstition.

There were long barrows all over the country, people walked past them all the time, and, as far as he knew, not one person had ever come to harm. No, he intended to farm the land as he saw fit.

Months went by, business was good, the crops were growing, and the farmer had long forgotten about the childish stories he'd been told. One day, at sunset, he was erecting a fence close to the long barrow when he became aware that he was being observed. A man with wiry, rust coloured hair and a fox-like snout of a nose stood atop the barrow, staring at the farmer with an angry frown. Naturally, the farmer didn't take kindly to seeing a stranger on his land, and so he approached the man and asked him his business.

"You're making a dreadful racket there, farmer," *the man said. "And those nails you're using must be made of iron, for I have the most awful chills running through my body. So, if I might be so bold as to offer a piece of advice, you'd do well to stop what you're doing, take that fence down, and be about your day."*

"I didn't ask for your advice, thank you kindly," *the farmer replied, feeling his temper rise at the*

cheek of this demand. "And as the landowner, I might ask you what gives you the right to tell me my business?"

"Landowner, is it?" the man chuckled. "My kin have lived on this land for thousands of years. You are but a tenant, Sir, and after you are naught but dust and bones, we shall remain."

"Tenant?" the farmer thundered. "I have legal documents that prove this land is mine!"

"Documents that mean little to us, farmer," the man said. "For we recognize a different authority to yours."

"Those documents are recognized by none other than Her Majesty, Queen Victoria," the farmer scoffed. "Your monarch and ruler of all in this land, so you would do well to take heed!"

The man shrugged.

"So be it," he said. "You've had your warning, farmer, I wish you well."

With that, the man disappeared behind the long barrow, and the farmer angrily returned to his work, determined to forget the matter.

Yet shortly after this incident, the farmer's luck began to change. His crops became afflicted with a dreadful fungi that caused the stalks to become brittle as bones and die where they stood. His cattle and sheep came down with a mysterious malady, their stomachs swelling until they keeled over and died. The winter hay stores caught fire and the barn holding them was razed to the ground. Slowly but surely, the farmer's finances began to dwindle to the point where every week brought a new demand from his creditors. At his wits' end, the farmer remembered his curious encounter with the fox-like man at the long barrow, and with no other recourse available, one cold, starlit midwinter night, he found himself standing alone at the very same place.

"Come out and show yourself if you are there, Sir, for I fear I may have vexed you and your people, and I wish to make amends."

Sure enough, the man with the fox-like features emerged from the shadows that pooled at the base of the barrow.

"Salutations of a dark winter's night, farmer," the man replied. "How may I be of service?"

The farmer explained his troubles and after apologizing for any offence given, enquired as to whether there might be some agreement they could come to that might reverse his fortunes and bestow bounty on the farm once again.

"Why of course, farmer, I'll be happy to help," the man said. "All I need is your hand."

Sighing with relief, the farmer stretched out his hand for the man to shake.

"I thank you, Sir, and am mightily glad to have ended our quarrel!"

Yet the man made no attempt to grasp the farmer's proffered hand. Instead, he chuckled softly, a sly grin spreading across his face.

"I fear you misunderstand me, farmer. When I say, all I need is your hand, I mean your hand."

And with that the small man's expression darkened and he drew out a twisted, blackened blade, which looked as if it had been cast from ancient thorn.

Stammering, the farmer backed away, an expression of terror on his face.

"Why, you must be confused, Sir! You mean to cut my hand from my body?"

"Yes, I do," the man said, as if it were the most reasonable request in the world. "You must make amends for our trouble with the very hand that has splintered the trees and cut down our hawthorn and hammered wicked iron spikes into the ground, which cause us no end of strife."

Struck with fear, the farmer stumbled off into the night, fleeing across furrow and field, hurling himself through hedgerows, paying no heed to the thorns that tore his skin, such was his terror. He only rested when he had reached the farmhouse and driven home the bolt on the lock. In the morning, he wondered whether he had had some wicked nightmare, and ascribed his midnight conversation with the fox-like man to some malady brought about by stress.

Yet, his fortunes continued to decline. The land grew barren and bare. The only thing to be seen in his fields were the yellowed skeletons that once belonged to his cattle and sheep. A mighty storm caused a tree to come crashing down on his farmhouse, and when the farmer retrieved his insurance documents, he discovered that he had failed to renew them and no financial relief was available. Shunned by the villagers, who believed him to have been put under an evil faery curse, the farmer sat alone in his ruined farmhouse, the winter snows pouring in through the gaping chasm in the walls, covering his furniture and floors until it appeared as if both he and his surroundings had been carved from stone. His stores ran dry, the last of his winter wood flickered away in a puff of smoke, and the farmer sat alone in a cold house with only his dark thoughts for company.

Not long after, the villagers were awoken by the sound of dreadful shouts and screams coming from atop the farmer's field. Most huddled in their beds, crossed themselves and prayed that the hidden folk would quickly return to their cold palace beneath the ground. Yet the bravest gathered with flaming torches, knowing that someone had come to harm and that it was their Christian duty to help. With trembling limbs, they marched across the snowy landscape until the long barrow came in sight, and there they stood aghast, fear frozen on their faces as if they had seen the Devil himself. For atop the long barrow, the farmer stood, silhouetted by the moon, screaming that he had made good on his pact and demanding that the "barrow man" honour their agreement. As the farmer raised his arms to the sky, the villagers drew back in horror. For where the *farmer should have had two hands, they could see only one. The other lay by his feet, blood spread across the snow like a giant red rose.*

"To his right there loomed against the westward stars a dark black shape. A great barrow stood there."

The Fellowship of the Ring,
J. R. R. Tolkien, 1954

Chapter 6
The Barrow

Aveline passed the phone to Harold and waited while he read it. His reaction when he finished was similar to hers. The briefest flicker of fright. Raising an eyebrow, he passed the phone back to Sammy.

"And you think this long barrow is the same one in the story?"

Sammy nodded gravely. "There's only one long barrow in Scarbury."

"Creepy, but you know it's just a story, right?" Harold said with a shrug.

Sammy pursed his lips. Aveline could tell he was annoyed by Harold's casual attitude. She could only feel a cold, curdling fear; the image of the one-handed farmer burned into her mind.

"You might think it's just a story," Sammy said with a weary sigh, as if this wasn't the first time he'd had to explain this. "Except that time and time again, we're learning that stories like these are often based on real-life events. Like the Pied Piper of Hamelin, for example. Over one hundred children did actually go missing in Hamelin and that became the basis for the story. Or Atlantis. There probably was a massive flood that wiped out some city and that's how the story of this lost civilization came about. So, the more you know about these stories, the better prepared you are."

"You seem to know a lot about it," Aveline said, shyly, taking a bite of her delicious chocolate chip cookie.

"Yeah, I've always been interested in the supernatural and stuff," Sammy replied. "That's why I started the blog."

"Aveline knows a lot about spooky stuff, too," Harold said with a casual toss of his fringe. "So I think we'll be fine."

Aveline whirled around, feeling her cheeks grow warm. "I'm no expert, Harold. I'm just interested in it, that's all."

"You know about this stuff, too?" Sammy said.

"A little," Aveline conceded.

"A lot," Harold corrected through a mouthful of cookie.

Sammy pushed his large glasses back on the bridge of his nose and locked his large, brown eyes onto hers, his frown becoming even more pronounced, as if he were suddenly having to think about something of earth-shattering importance.

"What's the difference between a ghoul and a ghost?"

"Sorry?" Aveline said, even though she'd heard the question perfectly well.

"Do-you-know-the-difference-between-a-ghoul-and-a-ghost?"

Sammy spoke as if he were asking a five-year-old. Feeling a warm flush of anger, Aveline took a deep breath.

"A ghost is the spirit of a dead person. A ghoul is like an evil demon that hangs around graveyards and eats human flesh."

Aveline glanced at Harold, who gave her a sneaky thumbs up.

"How do you know if someone's a vampire?" Sammy asked.

Aveline shrugged. "They drink blood and have fangs."

"And?"

"They have no reflections," Aveline said, racking her

brains. "They hate garlic...um...crosses and holy water. They can shape-shift, into bats and wolves. And they can't come into your house uninvited. Some people say they can't cross running water either."

Sammy nodded, either approving, agreeing or both. But it seemed he hadn't finished yet. Pausing, he massaged his jaw.

"Another name for a lycanthrope?"

"Werewolf."

"Okay...um...do you know what Black Shuck is?"

"A devil dog in East Anglia."

"Poltergeist?"

"Mischievous. Throws stuff around. Hard to get rid of. Sort of like Harold only you can't see them."

Harold guffawed into his fist. He seemed to be enjoying their spooky quiz, his head moving back and forth between them as if he was watching a game of tennis.

"Sorry for interrupting," he said. "This is pretty entertaining, but are we going to go and actually see this long barrow for ourselves or is the Supernatural Smackdown going to last all day?"

For the briefest moment, Aveline thought Sammy might smile, as she did, but he stayed in serious mode.

"I just don't want to take anyone up there that doesn't take the subject seriously. That's how they catch you off-guard. I don't like dealing with amateurs."

"Oh, don't worry," Aveline said, hoping Harold would let it go now. Sammy didn't seem the type for jokes. "We're believers alright."

With that, Sammy gave a curt nod.

"Okay. Let's go then. But when we get near, keep your eyes open and stay alert. Faeries can look like humans when they want to. Trust nobody."

Harold raised his eyebrows at Aveline and grinned, but she ignored him and they gulped down their drinks. As Aveline's mum had already agreed to the "educational trip" to the barrow, Aunt Lilian agreed to meet them at home later, as she ordered herself another coffee and settled back down by the fire. Aveline and Harold followed Sammy out of the door. Although Sammy certainly came across as a little intense and humourless, to say the least, Aveline sort of agreed with him. When it came to the supernatural, knowledge was power.

It didn't take long before they were walking out of the village once more and into the countryside. The lanes were strewn with leaves, which whirled into the air like embers from a fire every time the wind blew. Sammy strode ahead, leaving Aveline and Harold having to walk fast to keep up.

"He certainly means business," Harold whispered.

"Let's just listen to what he has to say," Aveline whispered back. "It's important if we're going to find out more about my uncle. And let's face it, he knows a lot more about the long barrow than we do."

Soon, they came to a sign.

Scarbury Long Barrow.
Ancient Monument. ⇒

"Okay, not long now," Sammy said, with what sounded like a note of uneasiness in his voice. They climbed over a stile and onto a narrow muddy track that led up the side of a field. The air felt heavy and electric, and as they puffed and panted to keep up, small flakes of snow began to fall, like feathers floating down from a pillow fight in the sky.

Sammy had ploughed on ahead and waited for them to catch up. As they reached the top of the field, they climbed over another stile, and the trail snaked left, leading them along the edge of a wood. Twigs cracked beneath their feet. Startled wood pigeons burst through the branches in a panic of feathers and squawks. Bare silver birch trees stood stiff and white like skeletal fingers.

"It's just along here," Sammy said in a low voice.

And then, rising out of the ground like some grassy whale, they saw it – the Scarbury Long Barrow. It was oval shaped, long and fairly high, maybe the height of a bus. Huge grey slabs marked the entranceway, a doorway made of stone. Muddy pathways made by the curious ran over its length like scars. In any other landscape, it might

have been mistaken for a simple grassy hill. But here, on this otherwise flat hilltop, it had an otherworldly dimension to it, as if something huge was straining to break through the earth.

"Pretty impressive, eh?" Sammy said, darting nervous glances left and right.

"Definitely," Harold said, studying it from underneath his fringe. "How old is it supposed to be?"

"Around 4,000 or 5,000 years, something like that," Sammy replied.

"Wow," Aveline said. "Can you get inside?"

"No, the entrance is blocked," Sammy said. "And probably for the best, too. Here, I'll show you."

Together they went to examine the doorway, which allowed you to walk in a short distance before large rocks barred the way. Aveline pressed her hand against them, wondering if they might suddenly slide away to reveal dark secrets within.

"So are there, like, skeletons and stuff in there?" Harold said, who seemed to have finally accepted Sammy as the local expert.

"Yes, there were, once. Don't know if they're still in there though. Archaeologists found some remains when they did a dig here."

"I've seen a photograph of the dig," Aveline said. "Back in my uncle's study. I think he..."

But she trailed off, still unsure of exactly how her uncle was connected to this place.

They climbed up on top of the barrow and took in the view; a dark tangle of the wood to one side, and the hilltop stretching away on the other. Beyond that they could see across the valley to the hills on the other side. The snow was still light, but the fields had begun to look like they'd been dusted with ash. There was a large stately home off in the distance, obviously the residence of someone very important and very rich. There were smaller houses, too, cosy cottages with smoke rising from their chimneys like wads of cotton wool. The land felt so still and quiet in the midwinter, as if everyone was indoors huddled in front of a crackling fire.

Aveline took it all in, feeling the warmth of their climb begin to fade, to be replaced by a creeping cold that snaked its way past her scarf and settled beneath her skin. Flakes of snow landed on her glasses before melting and she had to keep taking them off to give them a wipe. She noticed Sammy did the same.

"Why are you so interested in this place?" Sammy asked, plucking a few blades of grass and throwing them into the wind.

"I think my uncle was interested in it for some reason. We want to know why."

Despite her reservations about sharing too much, Aveline explained what had happened to her Uncle Rowan and the reason for their visit. Sammy listened, his frown moving from puzzled to intrigued, before his face lit up.

"I know about your uncle!" Sammy said. "He's in my *Dossier of Disappearances*. Here, let me show you."

Sammy pulled out a battered folder from his rucksack and undid the rubber band that tied it together, keeping his hands pressed tightly on the contents so they didn't blow away. Leafing through a series of newspaper cuttings and pages taken from books, he pulled something out and showed it to Aveline. It was a local newspaper, obviously quite old, the paper cracked and yellowed, as if it might flake apart at any moment.

The Scardale Gazette.

But it was the main headline that made Aveline's stomach lurch.

Fate of Local Man Still Unknown.

Grabbing it, Aveline scanned the article. It recapped everything about Uncle Rowan's case, including some information that Aveline didn't know. Apparently, the very last sighting of him had been late in the afternoon, just before Christmas, walking away from the village. That was interesting, Aveline thought: where could he have been going – and why? Then there was a mention of the fruitless police search together with possible theories. But perhaps most interesting of all was right at the end – an interview with a local shopkeeper.

...Bob Andrews was one of the last people to speak to the missing man. When we interviewed him, Bob recalled their encounter. "Mr Jones never used to say much when he came into the shop. He was a quiet sort of chap, but I remember this time because he had mud on his boots and he trod it all over my nice, clean floor. He was terribly apologetic and told me he'd been working at a local archaeological site. I hope they find out what happened to him."

Aveline read this last part out to Harold.

"*Mud on his boots* – what do you make of that?"

Harold shrugged.

"He was an archaeologist, wasn't he? Sort of makes sense that he had mud all over himself."

"But it says right here – a *local* archaeological site!

Sammy, are there any other places like this in Scarbury?"

Sammy frowned and pushed back his spectacles.

"Well, there is a lot of history here, you know, churches and old houses. But I've never seen anyone digging at any of them. There certainly aren't any other Neolithic sites."

"It has to be this place," Aveline said, almost to herself. "That means he was here just before Christmas. And I bet I know *exactly* what day it was. Remember what I said, Harold?"

"December 21ˢᵗ," Harold said, picking up on her prompt. "Tomorrow is the midwinter solstice."

"Sammy, who else is in your *Dossier of Disappearances*?"

"Everyone there's a record of," Sammy said bluntly. "You know that story I showed you about the farmer? That's just one. There's a story about two girls going missing in the 1950s who were on a school trip to the area. And there was this man who'd been sent to look at installing new drainage ditches, and he disappeared, too."

"We've seen those already," Harold said. "They're on the wall in Aveline's uncle's study."

"We think he was investigating what happened to them," Aveline said, purposefully leaving out the part about the séance tapes. She didn't want to make her uncle sound weird, even if it was rather odd.

"Sounds like me and your uncle had something in common then," Sammy continued, returning his dossier to his backpack. "And that's exactly why I didn't want you to come up here alone. I needed to make sure you knew what you were getting yourselves into. Long barrows are said to be gateways to the land of the dead. They're creepy places. And if you let your guard down, well, you might find yourself making an appearance in my dossier."

"What an honour that would be," Harold said, aiming a smirk in Aveline's direction. She could tell that Harold struggled to deal with Sammy's seriousness. All he ever wanted to do was joke about things. Sammy appeared to be the complete opposite.

About to move the conversation on, Aveline paused. She felt uneasy for a moment, as if they were no longer alone. There was movement out of the corner of her eye.

"What is it?" Sammy asked.

"I think someone's watching us," Aveline said, in a low voice, pointing over towards the wood.

They heard a branch crack, like a gunshot. The hedgerow shook slightly, as if somebody had just pushed their way past it.

"I can't see anyone," Harold said.

"No, you wouldn't," Sammy whispered. "They keep themselves hidden."

For a few minutes more they watched the wood, but the only thing they saw was a thrush throwing leaves around as it hunted for worms.

"I think we should be going," Sammy said.

Aveline felt the same and she could sense Harold's growing frustration with Sammy, so she clambered to her feet. It was time to head back and think about what they'd learned.

Crunching alongside the wood, they reached the stile that led back down the field to the lane. As Aveline waited for Harold to follow over, she glanced back towards the wood. The hedgerow was trembling again although it could have just been the wind.

"Up the airy mountain, Down the rushy glen,
We daren't go a-hunting, For fear of little men."

"The Fairies" from Poems,
William Allingham, 1850

Chapter 7
A Mysterious Invitation

After leaving the long barrow, Aveline and Harold walked back down through the snow and told Sammy they'd call him if they found out anything more about her uncle's connection to the barrow and the missing people. Then, after he'd gone, they exchanged a few slushy snowballs before heading inside.

"That was worth it," Aveline said, shaking melting snow from her hat. "We know a lot more than we did."

"Well, we do and we don't," Harold said. "Yes, we probably know what your uncle was up to, but we're no closer to finding out what exactly happened to him."

"We know it's something to do with the barrow. And we know the solstice might be connected, too. We just

99

have to keep digging. Anyway, it was good to meet Sammy. I think he's going to be a real help."

"Bit of a know-it-all if you ask me," Harold scoffed. "And he had the nerve to call *us* amateurs... I mean, *really?*"

Just as they were untangling themselves from all their winter wear, they were startled by a loud, insistent knocking on the front door, followed by the sound of footsteps scampering away into the distance. Aveline opened the door and peered out.

She heard what sounded like a chuckle from somewhere along the lane.

Perplexed, she walked to the end of the path and looked down it, but there was nobody to be seen. It was only as she came back in that she saw something had been left on the doorstep. It was a sheet of paper. A breeze picked it up and it fluttered away. Aveline gave chase before clamping her foot on it and picking it up. It had a picture of a dancing skeleton on it, holding a top hat in one hand and what appeared to be a bone in the other. It gave Aveline the chills. Aveline had assumed it was paper, but it felt older, thicker and slightly greasy to the touch, perhaps parchment of some kind. Taking it back indoors, she read it with a frown.

FESTIVAL

OF THE

LONG NIGHT

20TH DECEMBER

SCARBURY LONG BARROW

F O O D
D R I N K S
M U S I C
G A M E S
G I F T S

ALL WELCOME

FESTIVITIES BEGIN AT 3P.M.

"Strange place for a festival," Aveline said, snapping a picture of it on her phone.

"Strange full stop," Harold said, peering at it with a frown.

"I think we should go," Aveline said.

"But we've only just come back. And that hill is steep."

"Yes, but this looks interesting. It could help our investigation. We could even ask the people there if anyone saw my uncle, you never know."

Aveline's mum and aunt were yet to return, so they helped themselves to the contents of the fridge and warmed up with a hot chocolate. Through the kitchen window, the snow could be seen falling, making the garden look less like a bare patch of earth in south-west England and more like the North Pole.

They'd only just settled back down in the study when they were distracted by the sound of the front door opening. A cold blast of air rushed into the room like an excited dog.

"Aveline, Harold?" her mum called. "Are you two home?"

"In here," Aveline called.

A moment later, her mum poked her head around the door, her cheeks pinched red by the cold. Snowflakes in her hair slowly melted until they looked like droplets of glass.

"How was the long barrow?"

"Interesting," Aveline said. "How was your trip?"

"Productive," her mum said. "The estate agent said they can get your uncle's house on the market in the next few days and it would probably sell pretty quickly. Houses around here are in demand, apparently."

Aveline looked around at her uncle's jumbled study. She'd hardly scratched the surface.

"What about all this?"

"We'll just pack it up into boxes and put it in storage. Better still, we can pay someone to pack it for us. I'm keen to get back home as soon as we can."

"But, Mum, we haven't even begun to look through it."

"Best be quick then, hadn't you?" Nodding to their empty mugs, she added, "Fancy a refill?"

With the offer of another hot chocolate on the table, Aveline and Harold joined her mum and aunt in the kitchen. While there, Aveline took the opportunity to ask her mum about the festival.

"Mum," she said, adopting her most innocent voice.

"Uh oh, prepare yourself, Lilian," Aveline's mum said. "Whenever Aveline says *mum* like that, it means there's trouble on the way."

Aunt Lilian smiled at Aveline.

"Well, Aveline, is your *mum* right?"

Aveline reached into her back pocket and showed them the flyer that had been left at the front door.

"I just wondered if we could go to this later?"

"Sounds like fun," her mum said, giving it a quick glance. "But have you been outside recently, Aveline? It's beginning to resemble Antarctica out there."

"It'll be magical," Aveline said. "Like being in Lapland or something."

"Like being stuck in the freezer aisle at Tesco more like," Aunt Lilian said. "My toes still aren't on speaking terms with the rest of my body."

"Can Harold and I go on our own then?" Aveline pleaded. "Just for an hour or so? We'll be back in time for dinner, promise."

Aveline's mum and aunt locked eyes.

"What do you think, Lilian?"

"More fool them, if you ask me, but you know what snow does to children. It drives them out of their minds. They have to be outside, rolling around in it and throwing it at each other – and it seems like a family-friendly event, so why not?"

"You'll take your phones?"

"They will never leave our hands, Mrs Jones," Harold said with a grin.

"And we'll call every two minutes to let you know our exact whereabouts," Aveline added.

"Okay, okay, I get the message," Aveline's mum said. "You can go, back by 5 p.m. though."

"6 p.m.?" Aveline said.

"5 p.m. And no later."

And with that, the deal was concluded with everybody having got what they wanted. Aveline's mum and aunt got to stay in the warm, and Aveline and Harold had permission to continue stage two of their investigation into the strange connection between Uncle Rowan and the Scarbury Long Barrow.

With a couple of hours to kill before the festival began, Aveline and Harold returned to the study. If her uncle's stuff was going to be disappearing into cardboard boxes, Aveline wanted to make sure she hadn't missed anything.

"You know, if we're going back to the barrow, maybe I should have a look at your uncle's books about faeries?" Harold said. "I spotted a few earlier."

"So, you're finally taking Sammy's warning seriously then?" Aveline said, raising her eyebrows. "He's not got you...spooked, has he?"

Harold shrugged.

"No, but, well, he does seem to know what he's talking about, even if he goes about it in a slightly annoying way. Back there I thought he might even out-spook you for a minute."

"Hmm, no chance," Aveline said with a grin. "But you're right. It's a good idea to do some more research. See what you can find."

Settling himself among the scattered books like a cat curling up in a nest of cushions, Harold hurriedly began riffling through them. Meanwhile, Aveline continued to sort through her uncle's things. After talking with Sammy, she strongly suspected that when her uncle had referred to *them* during the séance, that he was talking about faeries. Some proof would be perfect.

After a few false starts, she found something interesting in a bottom drawer – a collection of small boxes. Inside were what appeared to be historical artefacts that her uncle had either found or bought. In one, there was a Roman coin, alongside a handwritten note that said it was a silver denarius from the reign of Emperor Septimius Severus (AD193-211). In another, there was a small carved clay pipe, dated 1634, which had been found on the banks of the River Thames in London. In the third one she opened, there was a single nail. It was thick and made from blackened metal. Dry mud was visible in its grooves. Aveline prodded her finger experimentally against the spiked end. It still felt sharp. The note that came with it said:

Coffin nail. Iron. Circa 1700s. Oxfordshire.

"Hey, Harold, look at this," Aveline said, holding it up. "It's an *actual* iron coffin nail! Maybe my uncle found it on one of his digs?"

Harold glanced with an aghast expression.

"Did it come from inside an *actual* coffin?"

"I don't know. I sort of hope not though."

"Hang on," Harold said, turning his eyes back to his book. "You said it was iron? That could come in handy; listen to this." He read out loud. *"Talismans against faery folk include iron…"*

Aveline was reminded of something Sammy said, too, or rather, something he'd shown them.

"That story Sammy showed us on his phone, the one about the farmer who cut off his hand. The faery in that story didn't like iron either. He said it gave him a headache or something."

"Best keep the magic nail then if we're going back up there."

Aveline wasn't sure she wanted something in her pocket that might have been next to a dead body, but it did make sense to keep hold of it.

"Here, Harold," Aveline said, tossing him the nail. "You keep it. You've got more pockets than me."

Picking up the nail between forefinger and thumb,

Harold sniffed at it and grimaced, before stuffing it into his jeans.

"Anything else in those books that's useful?" Aveline asked.

Harold scanned through a few more sentences.

"Well, it does mention that they don't like salt or fish either. Do you have room in your pocket for a salmon fillet?"

"Coffin nails, maybe, but I draw the line at stuffing a dead fish in my jeans."

"Fair enough," said Harold.

He scanned a few more pages.

"What it says about faeries in here is pretty creepy, actually. It's definitely more along the lines of what Sammy showed us. People being tricked or lured away and never seen again."

"People suddenly disappearing," Aveline said thoughtfully. "Doesn't that ring a bell?"

"You think Sammy was right then?" Harold said it with a note of disbelief in his voice. "I mean, yes, we've seen some pretty strange things ourselves, but I'm not sure I can swallow the faery theory."

"Why not?" Aveline said. "It's like Sammy said. These stories are always based on true events. We know that better than anyone. I think it's pretty clear that my uncle believed it, too."

"Hmm."

Harold didn't sound convinced but the more Aveline thought about it, the more these strange stories from the past appeared to make sense in the present, too.

"What else does the book say?" she asked.

Harold traced his finger along another few lines of text. "The places where they live are sometimes referred to as *hollow hills*. Some people say they're entrances to the underworld, so Sammy was right about that, too. Maybe the Scarbury Long Barrow is one of these hollow hills?"

Something about the term made Aveline grow cold inside. It made her think of dark, hidden places where people could get trapped...and lost. But then she reminded herself that they would be at a festival and surrounded by people and music.

They'd be fine.

Aveline returned to her uncle's desk. She still had one more drawer to go.

Inside, there was only one item.

A small metal box with a tiny padlock on it.

It was labelled, *DO NOT OPEN*.

Aveline took it out and held it up in the air for Harold to see.

"We have to open it."

"Aveline, it specifically says, *do not open*," Harold said, in the tone of a tired parent. "Why in your mind does that translate to *this should be opened immediately*?"

"So, you don't want to see what's inside?"

Harold threw down his book and leaped to his feet. "Of course I do. Let's find something to break the padlock with."

A metal chisel in one of Uncle Rowan's drawers was selected for the task and, with a grunt or two, they snapped the fragile padlock open.

"After you," Harold said. "Might contain a booby trap."

Gently, Aveline opened the lid.

Inside was a pendant or clasp of some kind. It was silver and had a transparent oval-shaped glass cover. Beneath the cover was what looked like a tiny skull with red and black butterfly wings spread out on either side.

"Ugh, what is that?" Harold said in a horrified whisper. Aveline shuddered.

"I'm not sure I want to know," Aveline said. The pendant had a malevolent air about it, as if some kind of evil had been trapped inside.

"Imagine being chased around by a tiny flying skull."

"Feels bad," she said softly.

"Maybe that's why he kept it in a locked box?"

Aveline replaced the clasp in the box and shut the lid. The room seemed to lighten. Where had it come from? It appeared to be different from her uncle's other artefacts. For one, it had been locked and a warning had been put on the outside. Was Uncle Rowan worried that someone might open it? Or maybe it was simply very rare and valuable? That would also make sense. But she wished her uncle had added some kind of note to explain what it was.

Checking her watch, Aveline saw that they'd been in the study for longer than she thought and if they were going to make the start of the festival, then they needed to get a move on. They went upstairs to prepare. They knew it was going to be cold and so they switched into Arctic explorer mode. This meant wearing every single piece of warm clothing they had, layering on vests, sweaters, T-shirts, coats and scarves until they both resembled very lumpy and badly made snowmen.

"Phones charged?" Aveline said.

Harold gave her a thumbs up. "Check."

"Supplies?"

Harold pulled out some granola bars. "Check."

"Compass, just in case?"

Harold pulled out an old brass one they'd found in her uncle's desk. "Check."

"Good. I'm bringing this as well," Aveline said, holding up a picture of her uncle that she'd found in his desk. It was only a passport photo, probably one that her uncle had decided not to use because he had his eyes shut. But at least it had been taken more recently than the other one she had in her bag, which showed the two of them together. The passport photo would have to do. "Maybe I can show it to people and see if they recognize him?"

"He looks like he's fallen asleep," Harold said, studying the photograph. "I can see why it didn't make it into his passport. But, yeah, it can't hurt to bring it along."

"Alright then, I think we're good to go."

They had to repeat their checklist with Aveline's mum and aunt until they were finally given the all-clear.

"Don't be late, please," Aveline's mum said. "And text me when you get there."

"We will. See you later. And don't worry, we'll be back before you know it."

It had stopped snowing when they stepped outside. The skies were clearing and a feeble, pale sun staggered towards the horizon, but there was a creeping gloom that told them it wouldn't be too long before it was dark. Tomorrow was the winter solstice, after all, the shortest day of the year, and the sun would set earlier than at any other time. Scarbury was infused with an eerie blueish twilight, ice beginning to sparkle on top of the snow. The village's frosty lanes, houses and lamp posts gave it an old-fashioned feel, as if nothing much had changed there for hundreds of years. Aveline had expected to see crowds of people making their way up towards the festival, but the lanes were quiet and empty.

"I think most people will go up later," Harold said, glancing at his phone. "It's only half-past three. You know, we're probably going to be one of the first ones there. How embarrassing!" Pausing to readjust his woolly hat, he added, "Maybe we should see if Sammy wants to come, what with us being amateurs and all that."

"Good idea," Aveline said, pulling out her phone. She fired off a quick text.

**Hi Sammy, this is Aveline. Me and Harold are on our way
to the festival, want to come?** 🙂

There was no immediate reply, and the phone said the message hadn't been read yet, so she pocketed it and they continued on their way. Finding the stile, they clambered over and began their ascent again. Their breaths came out in cloudy puffs. Their feet crunched through the top layer of the snow like a fork breaking into a pastry. On top of the hill, they saw a glow of firelight and heard faint snatches of music, as if a radio station was being tuned in and out.

"Looks like the festival's started," Harold said. "Wonder if there'll be something nice to eat?"

"I think so," Aveline said. "It said as much on the flyer."

Just then, her phone pinged. It was Sammy, replying to her text.

What festival?

"THEIR Apparell and Speech is like that
of the People and Countrey under which
they live."

The Secret Commonwealth,
Robert Kirk, 1691

Chapter 8
The Festival of the Long Night

Frowning, Aveline tapped out a reply to Sammy.

The one at the long barrow? It's called the Festival of the Long Night. There's food and games and stuff. Should be good.

As they crested the top of the hill and began to skirt the wood, a rich aroma of roasting meat and woodsmoke filled the air. A large bonfire sent tiny embers spiralling up into the darkening sky. Aveline began to feel excited, yet nervous at the same time. Her phone pinged. Sammy again.

I've never heard of it and I've lived here for years???

Aveline replied.

Might not be a regular thing? But it's definitely on.
We've just arrived and it looks really good!!

Stalls had been set up in a wide ring around the long barrow, which itself had been framed with flaming torches, making it look particularly mystical and majestic. A band was performing, though their music sounded old-fashioned, played with flutes and drums and something that sounded like a bagpipe. A masked fire juggler wearing a crown of stag antlers tossed flaming torches in an arc, leaving trails of glowing orange in the darkening sky.

Everyone else appeared to be wearing animal masks, too, which made Aveline feel a bit out of place, as if they'd turned up to a fancy-dress party without making any effort. They could have at least mentioned it on the invitation. Someone in a fox mask stared at her before glancing away. A small boy – or man – in a hare mask scuttled across their path, giggling softly. Away in the distance, the horizon glowed a soft pink. Above it, the sky was turning an inky blue, the first stars sparking and sparkling like tiny shards of flint. It really did have a magical, festive feel to it.

Aveline glanced at Harold and smiled. "This is really cool!"

"I know!" Harold said, his eyes wide, trying to take it all in.

Aveline felt a buzz in her pocket.

"Hang on a sec."

It was Sammy again.

Just asked my parents and they've never heard of it either.

Aveline showed Harold, who shrugged.

"Well, we only found out it was on at the last minute.

Maybe they didn't deliver a flyer to Sammy's house? Anyway, it might not be Sammy's sort of thing. You know, *fun*."

Stifling a smile, Aveline tapped out a reply.

Well it's definitely happening. Harold says if you come up he'll buy you a toffee apple 🍎

"Alright, let's go look at the stalls," Aveline said.

The first one they arrived at sold books, which immediately caught their eye. The books were old and in terrible condition, so much so that they were afraid to pick any up in case they crumbled away into nothing. Aveline and Harold glanced at a few, though they seemed to be a particularly morbid collection.

Poisonous Roots & How to Use Them
Lunar Curses: A Manual
The Corpse Roads of England
A Beginner's Guide to Creeping & Crawling

"Who'd want to read one of those?" Harold whispered, aware that on the other side of the stall, someone in an owl mask watched them with dark, blank eyes.

"Not me," Aveline said, thinking some people had really weird tastes. She felt her phone buzz again. This time it was her mum.

How's the Christmas Wonderland?

Frowning, Aveline typed back.

What?

The phone pinged again.

The thing you've gone to in the village. Has Santa arrived yet?

Aveline tapped away.

The festival isn't in the village?

"Let's eat something," Harold said, drawing Aveline's attention away, though her mum's texts bothered her. Why would she call the festival a *Christmas Wonderland* – and what did Santa have to do with it? And why did she think they were in the centre of Scarbury village?

The flyer she'd shown her had clearly stated it was at the long barrow. She wondered whether her mum and aunt had maybe opened a bottle of wine.

The next stall along sold food and Aveline felt her stomach growl. Skewers of meat roasted over a small grill. Aveline leaned forward for a closer look before quickly recoiling back. Somebody wearing a bird mask with a tangle of red hair peeking out smirked slyly before reaching out his hand and slowly turning the skewers over.

"Harold, were those what I think they were?" Aveline whispered after they'd walked on a few steps. She'd seen something on the end of the strips of meat that looked suspiciously like small wiry tails, which the flames had burnt to a blackened crisp.

"I'm not sure," Harold said. "But probably best to play it safe and avoid eating anything that looks like a rodent."

Another text from her mum.

So you're not at the Christmas Wonderland thing you showed me?

Aveline replied.

**I don't know what you mean. We're at the festival of
the long night. At the long barrow.**

Just for context, she attached the picture of the flyer.
Her phone told her the message had been read so she
assumed that was the confusion cleared up.

The next stall was another strange
one.

It sold spectacles, which
immediately interested
Aveline, having quite a
few pairs herself, because
there was always room for
more. Only on closer
inspection, these were all
broken; the frames twisted at
awkward angles, their lenses cracked and
stained or, in some cases, missing entirely. They had tiny
labels attached to them. Aveline squinted at them.

Mining disaster, 1917.
Car Crash, 1954.
Mountaineering accident, 1923.
Train wreck, 1968.

Did these glasses really belong to people who'd been in terrible accidents? And if so, who would want to buy such a thing? Aveline shuddered. There was something off about this place.

Glancing around, it suddenly struck her that, while there were plenty of stallholders and performers, dressed in raggedy costumes and bizarre masks, there didn't seem to be any *ordinary* looking visitors. No parents with pushchairs. No kids being carried around on their dads' shoulders. Nobody dressed like Aveline and Harold, just out for a winter's evening entertainment. No sounds of enjoyment either. No laughter or whoops or yells filled the air. Just the slightly unsettling music and watchful eyes of hidden faces. She hadn't even had a chance to show anyone her uncle's picture. These people, whoever they were, had an intimidating air to them, as if they were all part of some private club.

Another buzz in Aveline's pocket. Another text. Aveline glanced at it, before reading it a couple of times. Her mum again.

That's not the same flyer you showed me earlier?! Not sure I like the sound of you being up there – come home soon?

Yes, don't worry, won't be long.

Then a text from Sammy flashed up.

I think you should get out of there. I've rung around and nobody knows anything about it. Leave now and I'll come and meet you.

"Hey, Harold, look at these…" Aveline began before realizing with a dreadful, sinking feeling that she was talking to herself.

Harold was nowhere to be seen.

"Harold?" Aveline called.

Above the music and the crackling fire Aveline could hardly hear herself, so it was reasonable to assume Harold wouldn't either. Trying to stay calm, she walked on through the festival. He'd probably just got distracted by something. She sent him a quick text.

Where are you?

Stopping, she looked around. There was constant movement everywhere she turned, people in their masks with their strange, dead black eyes and odd, jerky movements. It had a dizzying effect, as if she was being carried along on a wave of colour and sound. She tried ringing Harold next, but all she got was his voicemail.

As she glanced up, in the distance, she saw a red woolly hat with a curl of black hair beneath it.

Harold.

He was walking into a small tent that had been erected right next to the long barrow. Running to the entrance, she saw a pathway leading in. A crude, hand-painted sign had been hung by the door, painted in garish red letters.

LOST &
NEVER FOUND.

It sounded like a lost property tent, but something about the sign's weird wording made Aveline glance back, suddenly aware that maybe walking in here on her own wasn't the wisest decision. The sun had dipped below the horizon, leaving behind a bloody smear. The snowy fields sparkled with scarlet fire. Taking a deep breath, she turned and walked in.

The sounds of the festival died away to be replaced by an eerie silence. Aveline shivered, despite the heavy layers she'd put on. The air had grown colder.

"Harold?" she called. "You in here?"

The entrance to the tent was narrow and winding, the canvas walls rippling in the icy winter breeze. Brass oil lamps hung from the ceiling, throwing Aveline's shadow ahead of her, so that she appeared to be following a darker, braver version of herself. She'd expected to walk into a place where people could drop off personal items that had been found, like phones and wallets and handbags. But she found herself in a tunnel that seemed to stretch on much further than it should. The proportions seemed wrong.

A glance at her phone. The bars had all disappeared. Aveline didn't like this one bit.

But she wasn't about to leave Harold. She needed to find him and get home.

Glancing around, Aveline saw that every few metres, there was a poster attached to the wall. Aveline stopped to look at one. It was a missing person poster, though unlike any she'd seen before. Usually on things like these, along with the person's picture, there would be a detailed description of what they'd been wearing, their height, build, and so on. There would also be an appeal for information with a phone number to call if you knew anything. But these posters were very different.

They had photographs, but they were blurry and dark, as if they'd been taken in a cellar. And instead of a description, there appeared to be a warning.

MISSING.
JASON SKAHILL.
Went hiking on the moor.

Got too close.

Prying eyes get poked out.

The next one along was equally bizarre.

SHEILA MCMAHON.
HAVE YOU SEEN THIS WOMAN?
No? You're not likely to either.

On and on they went. The faded faces of people she didn't know stared back at her as if she were their last hope.

MARK BRAEBURN.
LOST.
Wrong place.

Wrong time.

Now forever silent.

Aveline shuddered. The messages in these posters weren't appeals for help. They were more like the epitaphs you'd read on gravestones, except these had a spiteful and threatening tone. They didn't even seem to be a poor attempt at a joke. They were just downright nasty, like something a bully would write. She felt as if she'd stepped into something that she didn't understand – and didn't want to. Even the air tasted bitter. The sooner she was out of this place, the better. She was about to call out to Harold again when a particular poster caught her eye.

MISSING.
ROWAN JONES.
Last seen not minding his own business.
Any information on his whereabouts
to be kept to yourself.
(Nobody likes telltales.)

The poster had a picture of her uncle on it that Aveline had never seen before. He was standing inside what appeared to be a stone chamber, an expression of utter bewilderment on his face. Behind his glasses, his eyes were wide and disbelieving, as if he were seeing something he'd never encountered before.

Aveline backed away, her breath coming in short, ragged gasps. The picture seemed to capture the moment before something terrible happened and while she didn't want to look at it, she couldn't tear her eyes away. With every step, the tent became more nightmarish, and with every passing second, the festival screamed danger. In the flickering light of the lamps, shadows reared on the walls and her earlier determination quickly faded, replaced by a cold emptiness in the pit of her stomach.

Then, somewhere up ahead of her, she heard Harold's voice.

"Aveline?"

His voice sounded distant, echoey and more than a little frightened.

"Harold! I'm in here, in the tent! Hang on, I'll come find you."

Darting along the curiously long canvas corridor, Aveline reached the end and saw that it split into two. Left or right.

"Harold, can you hear me?"

"Over here!"

Harold's voice swirled around her as if carried on the wind, but it seemed to come from her left and so she went that way. As she ran, the path grew rockier underfoot. Missing persons posters flashed by on the walls. There were so many of them.

"Harold?"

"Why are you running that way, I'm over here?"

Spinning around, she saw Harold standing a little way behind her. A flood of relief ran through her body; the only warm sensation she'd had that night.

"Harold!"

Harold's tense, pinched expression relaxed for a moment.

"Am I glad to see you," he said, jogging up to greet her. "I must have got lost. What is this place?"

"I have no idea, only, I know I don't like it," Aveline said, breathlessly. "I saw you come in here and followed you."

Harold threw his fringe to one side in confusion.

"You followed me? *I* followed *you*. And have you seen these creepy posters on the wall?"

"Yes, you've got to come and see this," Aveline said. "You won't believe it but there's one of my Uncle Rowan. He's been here, I know it. We were right, Harold, except I think something terrible may have happened to him."

Leading Harold back the way she'd come, Aveline expected to arrive at the point where she'd taken a left turn. But the tunnel kept going and going until, to

Aveline's horror, it ended in a flap of torn, muddied canvas that stretched out over a rocky floor. Beyond it, there was only a narrow tunnel leading away into the darkness. Aveline blanched. Attached to the raggedy flap of canvas that lay in a muddy pool of rainwater, there was one final poster.

VANISHED.
AVELINE & HAROLD.
Instead of taking the right turn.
They took the wrong one.
Now alone in the dark.

The picture showed the two of them looking scared and pale. Their clothes were the same ones they were wearing now. Harold's fringe stuck out in a raggedy shape from underneath his beanie. It looked as if it had been taken only a few seconds ago.

"What is that?" Harold said in a trembling voice. "What's happening? I don't understand!"

"Sammy warned us," Aveline said. "He said it was dangerous and just before I lost sight of you he sent me this." She held up Sammy's texts for Harold to read. "And then my mum sent me these, which are even stranger. She seemed to think we were going to some kids' Christmas thing down in the village. Whatever flyer she saw in the house wasn't the same thing we were looking at."

"Can you call your mum now? Or Sammy? Or anyone? My phone's got zero reception."

"Mine, too," Aveline said. "Quick, let's try the other way."

They ran in the opposite direction, now in the grip of full-blown fear. There were too many *hows*, *whys* and *whats* for Aveline's mind to consider right now. All she wanted was to feel the cold night air on her face and get back to a warm house and a mum asking her why she was late when they'd agreed she'd be back by 5 p.m.

As they fled back through the canvas tunnel, the lamps on the wall began to flicker. Grabbing Harold, Aveline pulled him closer.

A moment later, they were plunged into darkness.

"Soon after her death she appeared to her husband, and said to him, 'I'm not dead at all, but I am put from you now for a time. It may be a long time, or a short time, I cannot tell.'"

The Fairy-Faith in Celtic Countries,
Walter Evans-Wentz, 1911

Chapter 9
Unexpected Events

"Harold?"

Aveline held him tightly by his coat but she still needed to hear him speak.

"I'm alright, hang on, let me get some light in here." A second later, the light on Harold's phone came on. In its harsh glow, she could see how pale and scared he was. She suspected she looked the same. Right now, she felt encased in ice. "What's happening?"

"I don't know, but we need to get out."

"Okay, let's keep moving."

The phone only illuminated a few metres in front, so they walked slowly, their feet scuffing over the rocks.

"I'm sure the entrance was just down here," Aveline whispered.

The place they were in smelled of soil and stone. The air was colder than it had been all night. The sounds of the festival were gone. All they could hear was the chill *drip-drip-drip* of water. Aveline reached out and touched the wall. It was solid and unforgiving, as if beyond her hand there was a thousand miles of rock.

"This was canvas when we came this way before," she said.

Harold shone his phone on it. Streams of black water trickled down over the stone surface. Strange rune-like symbols had been carved into the walls.

"Except we're not in the same place we were before," Harold said in a trembling voice.

They edged forward, stopping in their tracks. Behind them, they heard the sound of far-off laughter, a musical chuckle that might have sounded pleasant in a warm, well-lit room, but not in the dark, creeping gloom of a cold stone labyrinth.

"Just keep going," Harold said. "We've got through other scary things before. We'll get out of this... somehow."

As they continued walking, their bodies stiff and tense,

the rocky tunnel narrowed, squeezing the two of them closer and closer together until they could no longer walk side by side and had to move in single file.

"Maybe we should use the compass?" Aveline suggested. "At least that might help us keep track of which direction we're going in."

"Good idea," Harold said, rummaging in his coat pockets. But when he retrieved it, and they shone the phone on it, their hopes were dashed. The compass needle spun around and around, failing to settle as it would normally do.

"Might be something to do with being underground," Harold said, feebly.

"But how are we underground?" Aveline said, knowing the answer even as she said it.

"The only thing that makes any sense to me is that we're in the long barrow," Harold said. "That's where the Lost & Never Found tent led. You know, maybe it's a *hollow hill* like the ones we read about?"

Behind them, they heard a cry.

It sounded a long way away, yet Aveline thought she'd heard someone call her name.

"Did you hear that?"

"I'm not sure what I'm hearing or seeing any longer,"

Harold said. "Maybe we both fell asleep at that festival and this is just some shared nightmare."

As their eyes grew accustomed to the gloom, they began to see the outline of the passageway they were creeping through. Harold flicked off his phone.

"Better save the battery."

Aveline struggled to hold back the part of her that wanted to scream and yell for help. She'd never been a fan of small spaces and the longer this went on, the more desperate she felt.

The cold had now made itself comfortable in the depths of Aveline's bones and no matter how tightly she pulled her coat around her, it did little to stop her shivering. She thought about what her mum and aunt would be doing right now. Probably beside themselves with worry. Had they called the police? Was there a team of uniformed officers already searching the area with tracker dogs and crackling walkie-talkies while a helicopter hovered overhead? In one way, she hoped there was. She just wanted to be found, wrapped in one of those foil blankets, and taken home for warm food and drinks. Aveline's fear was just beginning to turn into despair, when the tunnel curved around to the right and, to Aveline's relief, it began to widen a little. It also grew a little lighter, like an eerie grey twilight. Thin snatches of sound drifted through the tunnel.

"Can you hear that?" Harold said.

It was a bell, chiming softly in the darkness. In another place, at another time, it might have sounded melodic and peaceful. Here it gave them a melancholy feeling, reminding them that they were lost and alone.

"I don't like the sound of that one bit," Aveline said.

Yet, at least it wasn't silence and darkness. It was something. It was coming from *somewhere*. And that had to be better than where they were right now.

"Maybe it's the festival?" Harold said, giving Aveline a faint glimmer of hope. "We might have found our way back?"

That was enough encouragement to set them off running. The tunnel curved around, widened, and they found themselves entering an underground chamber. Ancient tree roots coiled over the ground like serpents. The walls were made of earth. Set into alcoves, black candles sputtered and spat. On the walls, there were portraits, greasy and black with age and smoke. This didn't look like an ancient burial chamber any longer.

This was somebody's home.

Aveline stepped closer to look at one of the portraits.

It showed a bizarre-looking old man, his nose curiously long, like a snout. His hair resembled a bush that had been set on fire and his ears lay flat and pointed against the side of his head. Underneath was written:

Lord Hemlock, Lord of the Long Barrow,
Master of Traps.

"Traps…" Harold echoed quietly.

"Don't you think he looks a little like…a fox?" Aveline said. "Remember the story Sammy showed us, the man who wanted the farmer's hand?"

"Oh no," Harold said. "That *man* was a faery. An evil one. But he can't still be alive, can he?"

Aveline leaned closer, wiping a cobweb from the painting with the tip of her finger. She'd seen something she recognized.

"Look what's pinned to his chest."

Swiping his fringe to one side, Harold leaned in, too. Aveline heard him let out a long, slow breath. The man in the painting wore a very peculiar clasp on the front of his cloak; a small skull, with butterfly wings sprouting from either side, encased beneath a transparent, oval glass cover.

They'd both seen it just a few hours earlier, lying inside a locked metal box in Uncle Rowan's study.

"That's your uncle's," Harold said softly.

"You know, I don't think it is," Aveline said. "At least, I don't think it belonged to him. What are the chances of my uncle owning a clasp that looks exactly the same as this Lord Hemlock's? He must have found it here. I wonder…"

"You think it has something to do with him being here?" Harold finished.

"Maybe?" Aveline said. Here was a portrait of an evil faery wearing a very peculiar piece of jewellery that was now in her uncle's study. Aveline had been wondering if there was a connection between her uncle's disappearance and the barrow. Now there was proof.

They had a look at the next portrait on the wall. This one showed two young girls, standing side by side, both dressed in what appeared to be school uniforms. In their hands they held old-fashioned lanterns that burned with an eerie blueish glow. Below it said:

Mary & Fiona. Bearers of the Flames
in the Darkness.

"They look so scared," Aveline said with a shudder.

"Same names as those two girls who went missing," Harold said. "Remember the newspaper article on your uncle's wall? And Sammy's blog post about the lights that people have seen up here?"

Aveline didn't dare think what might have happened to them.

"And look at this one," Harold said, stepping to the next portrait.

This one showed an older man with an unhappy expression on his face, wearing overalls and carrying a large bucket of water.

Bobbity Bob, Lord Hemlock's
Water Carrier.

"The workman who disappeared," Aveline whispered. "The people who vanished – they must have been brought

144

here or why else would their portraits be on the wall?"

Harold was distracted by another portrait. He glanced at Aveline, then back at the wall. His face was ashen.

"You better come and look at this one, too," Harold said, in a shaky voice.

This one showed a man with glasses and a long beard. He had his hands held out in front of him and they appeared to be tied together by dark twine. He was looking down at his feet, as if ashamed of something.

Light Fingered Rowan –
Thief.

"Uncle Rowan," Aveline said. "He's here, too. He must be. He took the faery's clasp. They think he's a thief."

"Come on, let's go," Harold said. "I don't want to be the next victim."

Aveline stared at the portrait for another few seconds, wondering just what had happened, before following Harold.

At the rear of the chamber, three tunnels led off in different directions. Right in the middle was a shrunken, gnarled tree, its black limbs twisted together in knots. It resembled a tree after a forest fire, charred and crumbling.

Hanging from the top of it was a rusted bell, which was now silent.

"Who was ringing that bell then?" Harold said, his voice trembling.

"I don't know," Aveline said, glancing fearfully around. "The wind, hopefully."

Nailed to the tree were four crude signs:

Tragic Outcomes ⇑

Unexpected Events ⇒

Unfortunate Occurrences ⇐

Sudden Demises ⇓

"I'm no archaeologist, but I don't think these signs are what you'd expect to find in a long barrow that's thousands of years old," Harold said. "And I'm not sure they'd invented candles or oil paintings back when they were doing ancient burials."

"No," Aveline replied, carefully studying the signs on the tree. "I don't think we're in any kind of human place."

"So you think...?"

"We're in some kind of faery lair, Harold, underneath the barrow, like Sammy warned us. That festival, the flyer, it seems like it was all part of one big trap. Probably cooked up by the faery in the portrait, that Lord Hemlock. Sammy warned us that people have been disappearing up here for years. They're on the walls. They were lured here, and my uncle knew it, too. He was on to them."

"So…those people at the festival?" Harold said with a puzzled frown.

"Sammy said that faeries can assume human form. Remember how we never got to see anyone's actual face? We were the only ones without masks on. Maybe they were faeries? Or maybe they weren't even real, like illusions or something?"

Harold grimaced.

"So which way should we go?" he asked, peering up at the sign with wide, frightened eyes. "If I'm honest, I don't really want to go anywhere in this place except *out*."

"Neither do I," Aveline agreed. "But we can't just stand here. We went left last time and that got us lost. I don't fancy a *Tragic Outcome* or *Sudden Demise*, so I suppose we go right?"

"*Unexpected Events* it is then."

As they headed off into the tunnel, it grew lighter still,

which, in one sense, was a relief. The same thick wax candles they'd seen in the chamber flickered on the walls. But who had lit them? And as they made their way further along, they saw doors, set into the walls, with heavy iron handles and a single candle flickering on the front of each one. It resembled a castle dungeon.

"Should we open one of these doors?" Harold said.

The sense of impending dread was like a claw slowly raking down Aveline's back.

"Um...I don't know," Aveline said. When she'd found herself in scary situations before, she'd always had a good instinct about what to do next. Here she felt powerless and deflated, as if she'd ceased to be in control of things. It was the same way in bad dreams sometimes, where the harder you tried to get away from something terrible, the worse the dream became. As if sensing her despair, Harold flicked his fringe away and looked her square in the eyes.

"Don't worry, Aveline, we'll find a way out," he said. "But we have to see where these go, don't we? They might lead to an exit."

Aveline took off her glasses and wiped the condensation from them. Harold was right. She couldn't give up before they'd even started. But there was a bleak and dismal atmosphere here that felt exhausting, as if all her energy and imagination was slowly draining away. She put her glasses back on and nodded grimly. If they were really dealing with faeries – and Aveline had little doubt they were – then their greatest strength was sticking together. She couldn't imagine the horror of being here alone.

"Okay, let's see what's inside this one," Aveline said. Taking a very deep breath, she opened the first door.

"Come away, O human child!
To the waters and the wild,
With a faery, hand in hand."

"The Stolen Child" from The Wanderings of
Oisin and Other Poems,
William Butler Yeats, 1889

Chapter 10
Old Friends

At first, Aveline thought that they'd found a way out. She felt a stiff breeze on her face. They were in the open air. But now the sky was blue, the clouds like white popcorn. She could see and smell the sea. This certainly wasn't Scarbury and they hadn't been in the barrow long enough for night to turn into day – particularly not on the midwinter solstice, the longest night of the year.

She was standing on what appeared to be a harbour wall, in a coastal village that seemed vaguely familiar. Small fishing boats bobbed around in shallow waters but she didn't see a single person.

"I think I recognize this place, but it's different somehow," Aveline said quietly, turning back to Harold.

But he had gone.

And so had the door.

All she could see behind her were fishing cottages and narrow, empty streets.

"Harold?" Aveline called, before adding under her breath, "Oh no, not again."

He'd gone, and wherever this strange experience was leading, it would be something she would have to face alone.

Aveline walked down the harbour steps, onto the beach, wrinkling her nose as she inhaled the pungent aroma of seaweed and rotting fish. Gulls cried overhead and Aveline felt the wind pick up, pushing her hair back from her face. From somewhere in the distance came the clanging sound of a bell, perhaps a buoy far out at sea being tossed about by the waves. The day darkened as the sun disappeared behind the clouds. Far off on the horizon, Aveline saw a bank of menacing clouds approaching. A storm was brewing. Despite the sense of growing danger, she walked closer to the water's edge, black waves lapping at her feet.

Then something caught her eye, just a few metres out.

As the waves broke into foam, something white flashed into view, before quickly disappearing.

It was a hand.

Aveline's breaths became shorter, and she began to back away. Where she could go and what she could do in this dark dream-like place, she didn't know. She had no idea what the rules were. But something told her to get away from the water and to get away fast.

Even as she felt her feet sink into the sand as she back-pedalled, somebody, something, rose out of the water. Long, dripping black hair obscured the face completely, before a bony hand reached up and drew the hair to one side.

Staring at her was a face from her nightmares. Huge, empty, dark eyes. A thin skeletal face. Strands of wet hair stuck to white skin like seaweed.

A woman. Or what used to be.

The nightmarish figure smiled; a crooked grimace exposed yellowed teeth, hanging loosely from a bony jaw. A voice, dry and brittle, the sound of screaming seagulls and splintering wood.

"Aveline, I see you!"

The figure strode out of the waves, moving faster than should have been possible. Like a crab, the figure scuttled up and over the sand and grasped Aveline's hands in hers. Aveline recoiled and screamed as slimy fingers wriggled their way into her palms and broken nails crunched down hard into her skin.

Trying to tug her hand free, she felt the woman's nails sink in deeper, and Aveline yelled out in pain. It was impossible to free herself; her hands felt like they were encased in concrete.

Yet even as she was yanked forward, she felt herself being tugged back. A moment later, she was free of the woman's grasp and heard a familiar voice in her ear.

"It's me! Stop struggling, you're safe!"

On hearing Harold's voice, everything went black. Aveline blinked, opened her eyes, and found herself back in the gloomy tunnel. Harold turned to Aveline, his eyes wide with alarm.

"What happened? I followed you in, but we were just in a dark empty room. Then you started murmuring and waving your hands around and you were yelling at someone to let you go."

It took Aveline a few moments to gather herself and catch her breath.

"It was so frightening, Harold! I was on a beach, and then this...creature...this woman, well, she was in the water and then she was chasing me, trying to drag me into the sea. Harold, it was Cora Poole."

"What? Cora Poole!" His face paled. "The thing that happened in Malmouth? The lady in the waves?"

Aveline nodded.

"But how could that happen?" Harold said. "She can't possibly be here in the barrow...can she?"

"Well, no. I mean, I don't think so. It felt as if I'd stepped into a dream for a minute, and right away I just had this horrible feeling that I was being...haunted by something."

Aveline thought it best not to go into any more detail. Harold was scared enough already.

"Umm, maybe we best not go through any other doors then," he muttered.

Aveline sat for a minute, until her breathing became even again. The smell of seaweed still filled her nostrils. What she'd just seen had been terrifying. But how had it happened? Was it some kind of hallucination brought on by the stress of being trapped in the long barrow? Or had there been a reason it happened – a sinister purpose and a dark magic that had combined to recreate one of her deepest fears?

"We have to try another one," Aveline said. "I think there's a reason I saw what I did, but I can't be sure unless we see where these other doors lead."

"Are you sure we should do that?" Harold said, his scared eyes staring at her through a tangle of hair. "Two minutes ago you were being chased by something horrible."

"But she isn't banging on the door, is she?" Aveline said. "Whatever is in those rooms, I don't think they can come out here. It seems...separate somehow. I've got a theory."

"And I'm your guinea pig?"

"Don't worry, I'll be right with you. It's important. We have to try and understand what's going on."

"Good luck with that," Harold said, but gamely clambered to his feet. "Okay, I'll go first this time."

Aveline followed. The next door along looked the same as the first.

"Maybe we should hold hands?" Harold said.

Glancing across at Harold, Aveline noticed a light flush on his skin.

"Just so we don't get separated," he said. "Last time you were in a very different place to the one I was in."

"Okay," Aveline said. She reached out and grabbed Harold's hand. It felt very cold, so she gave it a squeeze.

"Come on then, let's see what happens."

Harold pulled open the door.

They were in a field. Just like before, they were alone, with nobody else in sight. It was hard to work out what time of day it was. It could have been twilight or early morning. The daylight had a grey, bleak tinge to it, and a cold wind blew through the long grass. Aveline shivered. Once again, she had a horrible feeling that something waited for them, lurking just out of sight.

"Look over there," Harold said, pointing to what appeared to be the ruins of a house. There were what must once have been stone walls, but they'd fallen apart a long time ago. A wisp of smoke trailed into the air from somewhere within the ruins.

"We should probably go and have a look," Aveline said.

"I'm not sure we should," Harold replied. "I don't feel very good about this place."

Aveline knew what he meant. She felt ever so slightly sick, too, but she also knew that this was something they had to face if they were to ever work out what was going on.

"Come on," Aveline said, giving Harold's hand a tug. "If we stick together we'll be fine."

From far off in the distance, they heard what sounded like a church bell. It tolled once, then fell silent. Aveline knew that bells were beginning to spell danger, but she stayed quiet and continued walking.

They reached the ruins a few moments later. Aveline stepped over one of the walls and into the interior. In the middle of what possibly used to be a living space, a small circle of blackened stones had been formed. Inside, logs smouldered, sending up the thin plumes of smoke they'd seen. To Aveline, it felt very unsettling. There was something not quite right about it. As if it had been prepared especially for them.

"Hello?" Harold called out. "Anyone home?"

Their only reply was silence. Aveline tightened her grip on Harold's hand. They wandered towards the back of the ruins. A large sign hung askew on the rear wall.

Private Property: No Trespassing.

"That's strange," Harold said. "Doesn't seem like anyone would care much about people wandering through a pile of rubble."

There was only one doorway still left standing. By the looks of it, it led into what could be a small storage room or outhouse. It was dark inside. Then, they heard humming; a breezy *la-la-la* coming from inside like a small girl playing with a toy.

"Hello? Is someone in there?" Harold called out.

The humming stopped.

A second later, a figure stepped into the doorway. The gloom made it impossible to make out who it was, but they could see the silhouette of long hair. A youngish girl by the looks of it. Aveline shivered. Something about the figure made her immediately nervous.

"Hello…um…who are you?" Harold said.

Eyes glinted in the darkness.

"Look at you two," a cold voice said. "Hand in hand, how cute. Finally found yourself a girlfriend then, Harold?"

Then the girl stepped into the light. She had curious eyes. One blue. One green.

It was a girl they both knew. Hazel Browne. A witch. A very dangerous one at that. They'd last seen her when Aveline and Harold were on holiday together in a village called Norton Wick. They'd barely escaped her clutches. Since then, Aveline had made a firm vow never to get close to her again.

"Hazel, what are you doing here?" Aveline whispered.

"Oh, a friend of mine asked me to come over and say hello to you both," Hazel said. "He's a wicked old thing, but I find him entertaining enough, so I agreed to come along. Thought I'd come and hang around the old house for a while and wait for you both to come sticking your nose in where it's not wanted. Seems neither of you have learned your lesson, have you?"

Her eyes flickered to Aveline.

"We're not doing this for fun," Aveline said, taking the bait. "We've been trapped here."

"Well, yes, that is his speciality, as I remember." Then Hazel turned her attention to Harold, her mismatched eyes narrowing as they sought him out. "I see Boy Wonder is still tagging along."

"You better not try anything," Harold said. Aveline winced as Harold's grip grew tighter.

"Or what, Harold?" Hazel said scornfully. "What are you going to do, *Book Boy*? Read me to death?"

Hazel laughed a sneering chuckle that was all hurt and no humour.

"No, actually, I don't need to do anything," Harold said. "I feel sorry for you. You're lonely and you're angry and you're jealous of people who are happy."

"You should shut your mouth, Harold," Hazel warned.

"Why should I?" Harold snapped. "We're trapped in here and we've had just about enough…"

"Harold," Aveline whispered.

"…and now we've been led here because someone is

trying to scare us, but you know what? I'm not scared of you, not one little bit. You're just a—"

"Enough!" Hazel cried. She stepped forward, then slowly raised her arms. A fierce gust of wind blew in, sending leaves flying into the air like a swarm of huge flies.

"I think it's time someone shut your mouth for good, Harold," Hazel smiled, before slowly drawing her hand across the lower half of her face.

Aveline heard Harold grunt. She glanced across and saw a look of utter panic in his eyes.

Where his mouth had been, there was now only smooth flesh.

Harold released Aveline's grip and scrabbled at his face. Aveline knew she had to act now. She couldn't allow them to become separated and she had to get them out of this nightmare.

Pulling his hand away from his face, Aveline yanked him back towards where they'd come in.

"Leaving already, Aveline?" Hazel called. "But we still have so much catching up to do!"

Aveline didn't listen. She knew what was happening now. Or at least she thought she did. She'd seen a spectre that had haunted her in the past. And now Hazel was trying to bewitch them. These were fears that she had faced previously – and overcome – but that didn't mean the fear had ever left her. And somehow, whatever lived in the long barrow knew this. It appeared to have the ability to reach into their minds and actually mould something real from what it found there. That was why Harold hadn't seen Cora Poole. She only lived in Aveline's fears.

Aveline didn't know if these long-buried terrors could actually hurt them – and right now she didn't want to hang around to find out. Glancing back, she saw Hazel rise into the air and Aveline knew that if Harold still had a mouth, he'd be screaming. Aveline dragged him towards the collapsed doorway, narrowing her eyes as she fought her way through the blizzard of leaves and dust. Stepping through, she closed her eyes tightly. If the barrow had used her mind to bring Hazel here, maybe she could use it to send her away? She cast her thoughts back to when she'd faced down Hazel before. The feeling of triumph. The sense of relief.

When she opened her eyes again, cool air blew against her face. A faint grey light glowed. They were back in the long barrow. Harold sank to his knees beside her and held his hands to his mouth. His eyes were wide from fright.

Gently, Aveline reached down and pulled his hands away, seeing, with more than a little relief, that his mouth was exactly where it should be – right below his nose, just above his chin.

"It's okay, you're fine, no lasting damage," Aveline said with a smile.

Harold frantically ran his hand over his mouth. Tugging on his lips, he pushed his fingers inside and ran them over his teeth.

"Never thought I'd be sho happy to shee my mouth," he mumbled.

"I'm sorry," Aveline said. "That must have been horrible."

Harold finally took his fingers out of his mouth and gave Aveline a weak smile.

"I can feel my heart thumping through four layers of clothes," he said, holding a hand to his chest. "Is your theory that we're stuck in a place where we're going to end up getting scared to death?"

"Actually, that's not far off," Aveline said. "I think the faeries are mining what's in our heads. They know we're scared and they're feeding on that fear. Like, it makes them more powerful maybe? Somehow they're able to pull out all the bad stuff that we've hidden away in our minds and then use it against us."

"I've got plenty in mine; we'll be here for ever," Harold grimaced.

But it gave Aveline an idea.

"Well, what if we think of good things? That way, they might not be able to see our fears. You know, try and forget we're terrified for a moment?" she suggested.

"That's probably easier said than done," Harold said. "But it's worth a shot. In fact, right now, anything's worth a shot. What's something good that you'd like to think about?"

Aveline thought about it.

"How about an escape plan?"

Harold smiled.

"Why didn't I think of that?"

"I'm serious. The main reason we got into this is because I thought we might find out something about my Uncle Rowan. And we were right. He is in here, somewhere. So I'm going to think about him. Then once we find him, we can think about getting out."

Harold nodded to the next door in the tunnel.

"After you then. I went first last time and nearly ended up without a mouth. Can't tell you how much I'm looking forward to never seeing Hazel Browne again."

Retrieving the passport photograph of her uncle, which she'd brought in her coat pocket, Aveline stared at it, trying to make Uncle Rowan her sole thought. She let her eyes suck in all the detail she could. His long beard. Those thin, wire glasses that looked so out of date. She thought of his house. The musty smell of leather and wood in his study. His crystals, books and art. The pots and pans in his kitchen. His walking stick and boots. The creaking staircase. The ticking clock. The dusty mirror. Every detail she could muster.

"Okay, I'm ready, come on," Aveline said.

But just as she was about to place her hand on the next door handle, they heard a faint voice cry out from behind them.

"Aveline, is that you?"

"They stole little Bridget, For seven years long;
When she came down again,
Her friends were all gone."

"The Fairies" from Poems,
William Allingham, 1850

Chapter 11
A Pinch of Salt

Jerking her head around, Aveline looked to where the voice had come from. A small figure stood silhouetted in the tunnel.

"Sammy!" Aveline and Harold said in unison.

They ran to him. Sammy looked at each of them with obvious relief. Sweat on his forehead gave his skin a coppery sheen and he had a panicked, frozen look on his face. Watery streaks ran down though the dust on his cheeks.

"How did you get in here?" Aveline said.

"I came looking for you two, and I saw you run into that weird tent. Then the next thing I knew, I was lost."

Aveline noticed that Sammy's calm seriousness had

gone, replaced by the same terror they'd been experiencing.

"Are you okay?" Aveline asked. "What happened to you?"

Sammy cast a nervous glance over his shoulder, as if to reassure himself that he wasn't being pursued.

"I was panicking. I couldn't find my way back and then I saw a door. So I opened it, thinking it might be the way out. But it was horrible. Suddenly I was back in my old classroom. Only, there was someone in there with me... a boy...John Shawcross. I remembered him. He used to tease me all the time and make fun of me behind my back. Used to call me Scaredy-Cat Sammy just because he'd seen me reading a ghost book once and—"

Sammy took his glasses off and wiped his eyes. "I'm sorry, I used to hate going to school when he was there. I was terrified of him."

"It's okay, Sammy," Harold said, patting him on the shoulder. "We both made exactly the same mistake, if it makes you feel any better. And we saw some horrible things that we thought we'd forgotten about, too. Aveline thinks it's the faeries, climbing inside our heads and pulling out all the things that scared us in the past."

"I don't care; I just want to go home," Sammy said,

looking at each of them with fearful eyes, as if they were silently judging him. "You know, I talk about this supernatural stuff all the time, but I'm actually really afraid of the dark. I always have been. I can't stand it in here, and I'm frightened of what I might see next."

Sammy wiped his eyes once more. He took off his glasses and rubbed them on the sleeve of his coat.

"You're not alone any more, Sammy," Aveline assured him. "We're here now and we're all going to stick together until we find a way home – alright?"

Harold glanced down at Sammy's coat and frowned. "What's that big lump?"

Sammy pulled up the hem. A large bag of salt was attached to the inside.

"Salt," Sammy said. Seeing the confusion on Aveline and Harold's faces, he paused and touched it reverently, as if it were made of gold. "Sea salt to be precise. Found it my parents' kitchen. I brought it with me, just in case."

"Are you going to rustle up some tasty dishes while you're here?" Harold asked.

For the first time since they'd met him, Sammy laughed, and for a brief moment, it was as if the roof had opened up and the summer sun was shining down on them.

"No, of course not," Sammy said, wiping his eyes. "It's for protection."

"Faeries don't like it, remember, Harold?" Aveline said. "We were reading about it before we came up here."

"Is there anything I know about the supernatural that you don't already know?" Sammy said.

"Not a lot," Harold said with a grin.

Sammy appeared a little calmer now. Aveline touched him on the arm.

"I'm sorry you got trapped here, Sammy, but I'm glad you're with us. It was really brave of you to come and look for us. If we're going to get out of this, then we need people here who know something about what might be going on. And nobody knows more about Scarbury Long Barrow than you."

Sammy pulled himself up a little straighter and pushed his shoulders back. And suddenly Aveline didn't feel quite so worried about him as she had a few minutes earlier.

"Go back to what you were doing before, Aveline," Harold said. "You know, thinking about your Uncle Rowan."

Harold explained their idea to Sammy, who nodded.

"I think it's worth a try. From what I've seen and read, we're in a place where the rules are very different. So maybe we can make up a few of our own? Go on, Aveline, see what happens."

"Okay."

Quietening her mind and pulling out the passport photograph, she held it out for the boys to see.

"Okay, we all need to concentrate on this picture," she said. "Fix it in your mind and don't let any other thoughts in, alright?"

They nodded and for the next few moments they all stared at the picture, foreheads creased in concentration. Once Aveline was happy that they had Uncle Rowan's picture embedded in their mind, she opened the next door.

This room was pitch black. There were no candles to light it, so Aveline flicked on her phone and turned on its torchlight.

"You still with me?" she whispered.

"Right behind you," Harold said, tugging the bottom of her coat.

"I'm here," echoed Sammy.

The light from her phone didn't reach far and did little to push back the shadows that seemed to stretch out towards her. This room appeared similar to the rest of the long barrow. A blend of cold rock and soil underfoot, with tree roots that curled up the walls and over the ceiling. As she advanced a couple of steps, she heard a shuffling sound.

"Did you hear that?" she asked, quietly.

"Yes," Harold and Sammy replied.

Taking reassurance from knowing the boys were behind her, and that Harold had her coat in a tight grip, she took another few steps.

"Hello," she said, raising her phone as high as she could. "Is anyone in here?"

A voice spoke from the darkness.

"Aveline?"

Stopping dead in her tracks, Aveline glanced back at Harold and Sammy, their eyes wide in disbelief.

"Yes, I'm Aveline," she said, feeling a glimmer of hope. "Who's that?"

Something moved in the gloom, just ahead of the light from her phone.

"It's me," the voice said.

A figure stepped forward and Aveline felt her legs wobble beneath her.

"Uncle Rowan!"

He hadn't aged a day. He still wore his beard long and those wire-framed spectacles. Behind his glasses, his eyes were closed, as if he were meditating. It was hard to make out what he was wearing. His clothes were entirely black, so much so that they melted into the darkness of the room until his head almost appeared to be disembodied. It was an unnerving optical illusion.

"Hello, Aveline, it's good to see you," Uncle Rowan said.

For a moment, Aveline was lost for words. She'd been hoping for this moment, but in her heart of hearts, she had doubts it would ever happen. But now she'd done it. Against all the odds, she'd found him. A great surge of hope and happiness flooded through her.

"Oh, uncle, I can't believe we've actually found you!"

Aveline stepped forward to give her uncle a hug, but he took a step back. Aveline wondered if he was shy, or perhaps something terrible had happened to make him afraid. It must be a shock for him, seeing a niece he hadn't seen since she was little.

"Yes, well done, Aveline, you've found me," her uncle said.

"Are you okay? We've been looking all over for you."

"Yes, I'm fine," Uncle Rowan replied, stiffly. He still hadn't opened his eyes. Aveline wondered whether it was because he'd been kept in the dark for a long time. She lowered her phone a little, in case the light from it was hurting him.

"What happened, uncle, did the faeries kidnap you? You've been gone so long – where are we? Wh – what is this place?"

Her uncle's jaw twitched, as if he'd just crunched down on something unpleasant.

"We're in the beautiful grey twilight that stretches on for ever."

Aveline frowned and pushed back her glasses. From what she'd experienced so far, there was nothing beautiful about it – the barrow was simply a horrible dark nightmare. But then she remembered what her mum had said about her uncle being a little eccentric. Probably just a strange turn of phrase. As if hearing her thoughts, Harold leaned forward and whispered in her ear.

"I'm not sure about this, Aveline. Something's not quite right."

"It's fine," Aveline whispered back. "Remember, he's been in here for years."

"It's so wonderful to see you in here," Uncle Rowan said, shuffling back and forth so awkwardly it seemed he'd forgotten how to use his feet. "I'm relieved you were able to find me."

Eyes still closed.

Then it struck Aveline. How did he know it was her when she came in? He hadn't seen her in nearly ten years and he hadn't even opened his eyes to look at her. Of all the people who might come looking for him, surely Aveline wouldn't have been high up on his list.

She pushed the thought from her mind. There would be a good reason. Right now, she didn't want anything to ruin this moment. She felt a little dizzy in fact. She couldn't begin to imagine how happy her mum and aunt would be when she brought Uncle Rowan home.

Behind her, she heard the sound of a phone camera. Turning, she saw Sammy peering at his phone screen, his fingers enlarging the picture he'd just taken.

"Um, Aveline, there's something wrong, I think," he whispered.

"What's that you say?" Uncle Rowan said, suddenly swivelling his head in Sammy's direction as if he caught a scent.

"He didn't say anything, uncle," Aveline said, slightly annoyed at Sammy's interruption. "So, how are we going to get out?"

"It's this way," her uncle said. "Come with me and I'll show you."

Uncle Rowan held out his hand, as if inviting Aveline to take it, which she did, recoiling a little at the frostiness of his fingers. She couldn't imagine how miserable it must have been for him, being down here, cold and alone all this time.

"Come on, let's go," she called to the others. "My uncle knows the way."

"Um, Aveline, we're not sure that *is* the right way," Harold said.

"Of course it is," Aveline said. "I think my uncle knows his way around this place better than you."

"Leave them, Aveline," Uncle Rowan said. "If they don't want to come then we can't force them, can we?"

"We can't leave them," Aveline said, glancing up at her uncle.

His eyes were still closed.

She felt a tug at the back of her coat.

"Aveline," Harold said, in her ear. "Look at him, it's not right."

"It's okay, Harold," Aveline hissed. She tried to focus her mind. Everyone was talking at once. Her head swam.

"There's no time to wait," Uncle Rowan said, his cold hand giving hers a tug. "We have to get going, there's no time to lose."

Her uncle's voice darkened, as Aveline allowed herself to be dragged forward. "Won't you open your eyes, uncle? Don't we need to see where we're going?"

Uncle Rowan's lips twisted into a grim smile. "It's very dark in here so I prefer to keep them closed. It's fine, don't worry, I know what I'm doing. Come on, follow me."

At that moment, Harold stepped up beside her. A second later, Sammy appeared on her other side.

"That's good," Uncle Rowan said. "Now we all get to stay together."

"I don't think so," Harold said. "Aveline's coming with us."

"What are you talking about, Harold?" Aveline said. "He's trying to help us escape!"

"Your uncle might help us escape," Sammy said. "But this isn't him, Aveline."

With that, Sammy raised his hand and Aveline could see that he was holding his big bag of salt. A second later, he began to throw huge handfuls of it onto the ground in-between Aveline and her uncle.

"Sammy, what are you—"

Aveline's protest died on her lips as she heard an unearthly scream, a strangled squeal of rage and dismay. With teeth bared, Uncle Rowan lunged at Sammy, before recoiling back from the thick lines of salt. Aveline watched in horror, her mouth wide open, as her uncle appeared to almost *slither* back into the darkness.

"Run," Harold said, giving her coat an almighty yank. Aveline's phone's light went out and when she flicked it on again, they were back in the tunnel. Breathing heavily, Harold bent over and rested his hands on his knees.

"Before you say anything," he said to Aveline. "Look at the passport picture of your uncle again."

Aveline drew it out and held it up close to her face. The *uncle* they'd seen in the room was the spitting image of the picture. Identical in fact. He'd even appeared a little faded, as if someone had brought the passport photo to life  and stuck it on top of a body.

"It…he was just a photograph come to life."

"That's why he didn't open his eyes."

"That's horrible," Aveline said.

"Smart move with the salt, Sammy," Harold panted.

"You know," Aveline said. "I sort of knew there was something wrong, but at the same time, I couldn't hear anything except his voice. It was like I was in a trance. I'm sorry…it's just…I hoped so much that…"

"It's okay, Aveline," Harold said. "Believe me, we're all disappointed it wasn't him."

"Then there's this, too," Sammy added, holding up his phone. "You two should take a look."

They crowded around it, the glow illuminating their shocked, frightened faces. Sammy swiped up a photograph, enlarged it, then passed it across for them all to see.

"What *is* that?" Harold said.

Aveline stared at it. She could see herself in the photo because Sammy had taken it from behind her. Opposite her was a small, crooked shadow, as if a dark winter night had been given form. They couldn't make out much detail due to the gloominess of the picture and its surroundings, but it appeared to a be a small figure, with a snout-like nose and a chin that jutted out like an anvil. Its spindly arms were stretched unnaturally, so that they were wrapped around the side of Aveline's head.

"Yuck," Aveline said, suddenly feeling like she wanted to take a long, hot shower.

"The fox-like man," Harold said, softly. "Lord Hemlock. There he is. We saw a painting of him, Sammy, and we reckon that he might be the same faery they mentioned in that story about the farmer."

"I knew it!" Sammy said, punching his fist. "The old stories are always right."

"Yep, you were on to him," Harold said. "And so was Aveline's uncle."

"This might have been going on for hundreds of years for all we know," Aveline said. "Luring people in who get too close for their liking. I mean, that's what happened to us, isn't it? We were drawn here by an invitation. And it was the same day all those other people disappeared. It's all connected."

"Probably," Sammy said. "I once read that the winter solstice is a time for dark magic, you know, being the longest night and all that. Maybe that's when the faeries are at their strongest? And now I'm possibly the first person in the world to ever capture one on camera." He muttered under his breath. "They're not going to believe it when I share this."

"Okay, well the good news is that Sammy has a great picture for his blog," Harold said. "The bad news is we're the latest in a long line of people who have been trapped here on the winter solstice and never escaped. Not to mention that we can't find Aveline's uncle or a way out, and our greatest fears are coming to life everywhere we look."

"Don't give up just yet," Aveline said. "Yes, it's like a nightmare down here, but look – we're still here. I think they can only use what we give them – you know, our fear."

"That might be enough, Aveline," Sammy said. "Because I don't think it's possible to not be afraid down here. And what if the longer we're here, the more they get to know what's inside our heads? Maybe it'll just get worse?"

"Well, then we best think of something," Harold snapped. "I thought with the top two supernatural experts in the country alongside me I'd have nothing to worry about. So if Aveline's uncle *is* actually in here – and I'm sorry, Aveline, but I'm beginning to have my doubts – then you two need to find him and get us out, sharpish. Because I don't know about you, but I seriously don't want to open any more doors."

"You know, I think I've got an idea," Aveline said. "What if all I did was put the *wrong* thing in our head?"

"I don't understand," Harold said.

"Well, last time, when I walked into that room, I was already feeling scared. All I could think of was what might be waiting for us inside. I wasn't...hopeful. And that passport picture didn't help much either, my uncle looks so weird in it. Hold on one second, let's try again with this instead."

Fetching the other photo of Uncle Rowan from her backpack, the one of them by the lake, she held it up for the others to see.

"Is that you?" Harold said.

"Might be," Aveline blushed.

"Cute. But why would this one be any different?"

"Well, it's like the passport photo wasn't really my uncle. It was a picture of him, yes, but that's all it was. This one's different. It's real life. I'm there, he's holding my hand, and we're exploring, so it's like you're really seeing him for who he is, rather than just a face. It makes me happy to look at it, and I think that might help."

"We can try it," Sammy said. "But if we run into another faery, we don't have any way of defending ourselves. The salt's all gone. My parents won't be happy next time we sit down to dinner."

"I suppose we've all got our feet so we can still run," Harold said. "And in all honesty, I think we're going to need more than some fancy salt anyway. Go on then, Aveline. But if this doesn't work then no more door opening, okay?"

Nodding, Aveline flicked her phone on again and held it over the photograph. This time though, she directed her thoughts not so much towards her uncle, and how he looked, but tried to focus more on their connection. They were family. They had a bond that joined them together. As she concentrated, she heard a voice chime inside her mind for a moment.

Aveline.

"...and it is said that a man went out of one of these houses at the wrong time, for when found he was dead: the fairies had taken him because he interfered with their procession."

The Fairy-Faith in Celtic Countries,
Walter Evans-Wentz, 1911

Chapter 12
A Reunion

The voice echoed away into silence. But it was enough to give Aveline a sense of direction. Turning away from the door in front of them, she beckoned for the others to follow.

"It's this way," she said confidently.

"How do you know?" Sammy asked with a frown. "All these doors look the same."

"Just follow her," Harold said. "She's on to something."

With Harold and Sammy close behind, Aveline set off along yet another dark and winding path, passing door after door. Stone steps led up and down, tunnels branched off in all directions, tempting them with alternative routes, but she ignored them and let her instincts guide her until she finally stopped outside a door. It didn't look any different to the others – old and stained, knotted and studded – yet somehow she knew this was the right one. She grasped the handle and pushed it.

The door swung open to reveal Uncle Rowan's study. Exactly as they had left it. It was lit by the same lamp on the same desk, but sitting at it was a man with a book in his hand. His beard was so long that it lay coiled in his lap like a sleeping cat. Behind thin, wire-framed glasses, glazed eyes peered back at them, hooded and dim like two lamps that had been turned down low.

The man frowned.

"I had a dream about you," he said eventually. "You were rooting about in my study looking at my things. Who are you?"

"Uncle Rowan!"

Aveline couldn't contain her joy. Despite the change in his appearance, she'd recognized him immediately.

"That's funny," the man said. "We share the same name."

"Um…no, *my* name's not Uncle Rowan," Aveline said, excitedly. "That's your name. And you know me, uncle, don't you? It's me, Aveline."

The man clambered slowly to his feet with a pained

expression as if he'd been sitting for a long time.

"Little Ave – is that you?"

"Yes!"

Relief flooded through Aveline and her mouth stretched into a wide smile. Turning, she grinned at the boys.

"It's him!" she whispered.

To make doubly sure, Sammy held up his phone and snapped off a quick picture. Looking at it, he smiled and gave her the thumbs up.

The man flung his beard to one side like a winter scarf.

"Hmm, yes, Little Ave. I did used to know somebody by that name, a long time ago. My sister's daughter. A sweet, young thing. But she's dead now. Fell into the sea during a storm. Lord Hemlock told me the bad news. Very sad. I seem to recall she was very bright, had a promising future ahead of her."

"But I'm not dead, Uncle," Aveline insisted. "I'm here, it's me, we've come to rescue you!"

"Rescue me?"

The man laughed, before lapsing into a wheezy coughing fit that went on for some minutes. When he finished, he wiped his mouth with his beard and stared at Aveline again, before nodding to Harold and Sammy.

"Ah, now I get it! Rescue, indeed. No, any moment now you'll all change into three little demons and start chasing me around my study. Or your skin will suddenly drop off. Or your eyeballs will burst. You can't scare me any longer. I've seen it all down here, my young friends, more horrors than you can imagine. My tormentor never seems to get bored. And I'm so very, very tired of it all. Oh well."

With that, he turned his back on them, sat down in his chair and began leafing through the pages of a thick, dusty book that lay open on the table.

"Is that really your uncle?" Harold whispered in her ear. "Why doesn't he believe us?"

"Something's happened to him," Aveline said with a frown. "And I have a good idea what. I mean, we've only been here a short time and look what we've seen."

She decided to try again and coughed, very loudly.

"Um…Uncle Rowan, do you know how long you've been here?"

"For ever and a day," Uncle Rowan replied, without turning around.

"Do you know how to get out? I know my mum and aunt…um…Susan and Lilian, they really miss you and would love to see you."

Uncle Rowan paused.

"My sisters?" he said.

"Yes."

"You must be mistaken. Both my sisters are dead. Lord Hemlock informed me about that, too. Said there'd been a terrible accident. A tree fell on them during a hurricane. Squashed like ants. Nothing they could do. Terrible tragedy, all of them, gone." Uncle Rowan snapped his fingers. "Poof! Just like that!"

Aveline stepped forward.

"But they're not gone, Uncle, they're alive just like me. We're all here and now we've come to take you home."

Wheeling around in his chair at lightning speed, Uncle Rowan's eyes grew misty for a second before he blinked and his face reddened.

"I don't know what you could possibly mean. I'm stuck here and that's the end of it. Now, if you really are children, then it's time you were off to find your beds or your treehouse or wherever it is you sleep. Lord Hemlock will be arriving soon, and I don't think you'll find him as friendly and welcoming as I am. He doesn't like children as I recall."

With that he wheeled himself back around and began

muttering under his breath.

Aveline clenched her fists in frustration. They needed to get away from here. Yet her uncle's behaviour scared her. It seemed obvious that he didn't quite have his wits about him, but she had no idea what to do about it. Worse, his frequent references to Lord Hemlock scared her even more. The portrait of the Lord of the Long Barrow was unsettling enough. The picture Sammy had taken was terrifying. If this was indeed the same faery they'd read about in the story, then every second they delayed, the greater the danger. They needed to be as far away from here as they could possibly get.

"Uncle…" Aveline said. "Please."

Taking his hands from his book, Uncle Rowan stuck his fingers in his ears and began to hum loudly.

"I think that's the end of the conversation for now, don't you?" Harold said.

Together, they huddled in the corner of the study.

"Looks as if he's a bit confused," Sammy said. "He's not making much sense, is he? What was all that about you falling off into the sea?"

"No idea," Aveline said with a gulp. "But it's pretty clear that Lord Hemlock is tormenting him."

When she first saw her uncle, she'd imagined this

would go very differently. He would turn, with tears in his eyes, gather her up in the tightest hug, then the four of them would make their escape from the long barrow. Her mum and aunt would cry and say how wonderful and resourceful and brave she was for bringing him home. Now she had no idea what to do. Yet, the fact remained that he was alive, and that gave her hope.

"Any ideas?"

Harold and Sammy's blank expressions told her everything she needed to know.

"We have to do something," she said. "We can't force my uncle to leave, and he believes I'm dead. He won't listen to anything I say. You heard him; he thinks we're some kind of illusion."

"We might have to leave him while we go look for a way out," Harold said, softly. "I mean, what can we do? I don't want to end up as a painting on a wall."

"Me neither," Sammy said, before adding, "Sorry, Aveline."

Aveline sighed.

"Please, let's have a think first. I'm not going to leave him. Not now that we've finally found him. We might never find him again if we abandon him now. There must be some way of bringing him back to his senses. It's like

Snow White when the Prince kisses her and she wakes up from her sleep."

"I'm not kissing your uncle," Harold said.

Just then, they heard what sounded like a thousand tiny bells ringing at once. It was followed by a large thump, as the book Uncle Rowan had been studying fell to the ground. His eyes widened when he saw Aveline still standing by the study door.

"He's coming!" Uncle Rowan said in a sing-song voice. "Lord Hemlock is coming!"

"The fairies are, of course, visible to them, and many a new-built house have they bid the owner pull down because it lay on the fairies' road."

The Celtic Twilight,
William Butler Yeats, 1893

Chapter 13
Lord Hemlock

Aveline, Harold and Sammy exchanged panicked glances.

"What should we do?" Sammy said.

"We should probably get out of here," Harold said. "And very quickly."

"I'm not leaving my uncle," Aveline said.

"We could hide in there?" Sammy said, motioning to the wardrobe. It was the same one Aveline had seen in her uncle's other study – the cheesy archaeology-joke sticker was on the door here, too.

"Oh, there's no hiding from Lord Hemlock, I'm afraid," Uncle Rowan said. "You're in his domain now."

"Then we're trapped," Harold said, glumly. "It's all over."

The clanging bells grew louder, as if every clock in Scarbury had started chiming all at once. Uncle Rowan grabbed his book, stood up, and clutched it to his chest like a child with a teddy bear, his expression veering between joy and terror, as if he couldn't quite decide how he felt.

Aveline wondered if there was anything they could do, running quickly through the options in her head. What truly terrified her was what her uncle had said.

He doesn't like children, as I recall.

Yet time had run out.

The bells stopped.

Aveline crouched in the corner of the study, pulling the boys down with her. Harold was right. There was nothing they could do.

After a moment's silence, they heard footsteps – cold, echoing slaps that grew louder and louder until they were almost deafened – as if a giant were stomping down the tunnel towards them. Uncle Rowan let out a quiet whimper and hurriedly began tidying his desk, moving pens, papers and books to one position before immediately returning them to the same place.

Slowly, the handle on the door moved. Aveline felt a sudden burst of panic. What would become of them?

They were like sitting ducks. But it was too late now.

The door creaked open. Uncle Rowan's face paled and he gave a quick glance in their direction.

A second later, a shadow crept in.

It fell across the floor first, before looming large upon the wall, where it began to spread like ink dropped onto a wet piece of paper. Aveline could see a head, arms and legs, fingers stretched out like daggers, an elongated nose that resembled an animal snout, and a pointed chin.

Uncle Rowan gazed up at it, his eyes wide behind his wire-framed glasses, his mouth voicing silent words. The shadow grew larger. The room dimmed. Aveline shivered. A clock struck out a single, booming, melancholy chime. Then, the shadow bent over Uncle Rowan until all they could see was his quivering silhouette. In the darkness, they heard a sibilant whisper, a slow hiss that froze Aveline's blood in her veins.

"No, I...um...I'm not up to any tricks," Uncle Rowan stammered, seemingly understanding what was being said.

The shadow stretched again, like a black yawn. Aveline could smell something rank and mildewed. Uncle Rowan shifted in his seat, as the low, rumbling hiss sounded again.

"Escape? From the barrow? No, no, how could I? You are the master here. I know, I've learned my lesson. But please leave the children...I could talk to them...make them promise never to come here ever again."

There was a low chuckle, a scathing, dry rasp that chilled Aveline to the bone. The shadow reared, like giant bat wings, its head swivelling in Aveline's direction before it swooped towards them. Squeezing her eyes shut, she held her breath, waiting for what, she didn't know, but she was terrified all the same. A cold, clammy gloom descended on them like a freezing fog. Aveline could feel Harold trembling beside her. In her mind, she began to see horrible things: bleak hillsides, the wind sweeping across them like a ragged cough; abandoned houses with broken windows, built from blackened brick; grim pools of glistening dark water with a white hand bursting out to clutch at the air. She heard a strangled cry from Sammy. She felt her chest tighten. A voice cried out. Her uncle's.

"Please, leave them alone!"

And she was enveloped in complete and utter darkness, as if a gloved hand had closed over the top of her head and squeezed.

At that point, Aveline couldn't hold it in any longer, and she screamed, long and loud, kicking out her fists and legs in an effort to break free.

A second later, a candle sputtered in the darkness, a bell chimed, and Aveline was suddenly back in the chamber with the signposts, sitting with her back to a cold, earthen wall.

And she was alone.

At first, all she could do was look around in horror. This had to be another one of those weird hallucinations. Surely, any second now, she would feel a reassuring hand on her shoulder, and she would turn around to see Harold and Sammy smiling.

And yet, it didn't feel like she was in another nightmare room. This one was horribly familiar. She could see the signposts nailed to the withered tree in the centre of the chamber. Turning, she saw the portraits on the wall. Only now, there was one more.

She climbed to her feet and went to have a look.

It was a portrait of her, except in the painting, she looked about a hundred years older. Her face looked withered and shrunk, her cheeks just empty hollows. Her eyes appeared white and unseeing, her hair lank, long and grey. Underneath it said:

Aveline Jones. Meddler.

It seemed to offer a terrible glimpse into her future – one which made her even more fearful for herself, as well as her friends and uncle. Was this to be her fate now? To be endlessly wandering from room to room, facing the awful terrors that lurked, locked away in the dark corners of her mind, until she was stuck in a constant loop of anxiety and fear like her uncle? Turning away, Aveline looked around the chamber. Staying here feeling afraid wouldn't help. She had to do something.

"Harold? Sammy?"

The candle hissed again behind her, making her start. It gave off a rank, sulphurous odour that made her head swim. Yet again, she faced a choice. She had no idea where the boys were, or her uncle for that matter. Would it be better to stay here and hope that they would find her? Or should she go looking for them? In the end, she went to the mouth of each tunnel and called down them.

"Harold? Sammy? Uncle Rowan? Can any of you hear me?"

Her only answer from the first two was silence. But at the mouth of the third, she heard the faintest of cries.

"Aveline! Help us, we're trapped!"

It sounded like Harold, but she couldn't be certain. The chill wind that blew through the barrow distorted everything she heard. But if he and Sammy were in trouble, and needed help, then she didn't have any choice.

"I'm coming!" she cried. "Hold on."

She ran down the tunnel, calling their names. Their panicked replies came louder now.

"We're in here! Help!"

Reaching another of the wooden doors, she pressed her ear against it.

"Are you in there?"

"Yes, we're caught in something and can't move!"

"Okay, hang on, I'm coming in."

Leaning her shoulder into the hard, unforgiving wood, she pushed down the handle and with a grunt, the heavy door opened.

She peered into darkness before light suddenly flooded the room, making her squint and shield her eyes.

Facing her was a stage made of wood. Its red velvet curtains were closed and a sign on the front said:

Lord Hemlock Presents:
Alone in the Dark. A Midwinter Drama.

"Harold?" she called, nervously, before checking behind her to make sure she could still see the door. It was there and she backed into it, taking hold of the heavy metal handle.

A bell began to toll.

The curtains opened to reveal scenery that had been painted to resemble the inside of the barrow.

Harold sat on the front of the stage with his head bowed.

"Harold?" Aveline said. "What's going on? Are you alright? Where's Sammy?"

"Sammy," Harold called casually. "She's here."

From one side of the stage, Sammy appeared. He walked awkwardly, as if he'd hurt his legs or something.

"What happened to you two?" Aveline said. There was something about them that disturbed her, as if they'd lost all their energy. "Did you see Lord Hemlock again? I just found myself in the barrow and didn't know where anyone was."

Harold sighed, before lifting his head slightly. One wide-open eye stared at her from beneath dark strands of hair.

"Your uncle is silly, isn't he?"

To Aveline's horror, Sammy laughed. He still hadn't looked up either, his head hanging on his chest as if it weighed heavily on him.

"You're not wrong there, Harold," Sammy said, his voice low and harsh. "Pretty easy to see why he got trapped here."

"Sammy!" Aveline said. "You know he's not the first person to get trapped here, it can happen to anyone. It happened to us!"

"Well," Harold said, one beady eye still fixed on her. "Really, it happened to *you*, didn't it? Sammy and I can get out any time we please."

"Yep, we only came along for a laugh," Sammy said.

"And seeing you running around like a headless chicken has been *very* entertaining, Aveline."

They burst into laughter.

"Wonder how long it'll take her and her uncle to find their way out once we leave," Harold snickered.

"Yep, all on her own and nobody to show her the way out."

Both boys collapsed into laughter again, their bodies shaking and juddering.

Aveline felt sick. No matter what horrible things they were saying, the thought of being alone in here without them was even worse. It was a fear she'd always had but never voiced out loud.

But these weren't her friends – were they?

She took a step closer to Harold and Sammy, who were still laughing hysterically. It was too much laughter, as if it was forced. In the gloom, it was hard to see exactly what it was, but something trailed from Harold and Sammy's backs up into the ceiling. Something that looked like a straggle of dark cobwebs.

"What's that on your back, Harold?" Aveline said, edging closer.

"What? I don't know what you're talking about," he sneered.

"I think you do," Aveline said.

The two boys leaped to their feet. And now Aveline could see them for what they were.

They were puppets painted to look like creepy versions of Harold and Sammy. The Harold-puppet's entire head was covered by coarse black hair. The Sammy-puppet's glasses covered his whole face, which had been painted like a skull.

They began to speak in squeaky high-pitched voices.

"All alone!" they chanted in unison, shaking their skinny arms to the ceiling. "Aveline's all alone!"

Aveline screamed out loud in frustration. She should have known better by now. As the Harold and Sammy puppets began to dance even more maniacally, she couldn't stand to watch any more. Grasping the door handle, she pulled down on it and let herself back out into the gloom of the tunnel. She knew it had been just another trick. But part of her did wonder if Harold and Sammy were having that exact conversation right now.

Well, in one sense, Lord Hemlock's trick had worked. A low, thin mist swirled around her ankles, and she had never felt more alone. She could still hear the insane cackling of the puppets from behind the door and, with a weary sigh, she set off walking, no longer caring if she was going in the right direction. There was no *right direction* anyway. Everywhere led to the same. To more nightmares and riddles and fear.

As she walked, Aveline's legs felt like icicles. Tears pricked at the corners of her eyes. How much longer could she do this? Her uncle had been here for years. She couldn't bear the thought of being here for another minute.

And yet she clenched her fists.

No.

She'd survived. These encounters were designed to drain her spirit. She knew that. And in one sense, they worked. She'd never felt quite so unhappy and lost. Yet here she was, still in one piece. Her uncle was here, too, and she had a chance to save him. And she knew the boys were somewhere here as well.

This wasn't how it was going to end.

She would stay and fight. Lord Hemlock could do what he wanted, but she wasn't going anywhere without her uncle.

That was when she heard footsteps.

"They are fairies;
he that speaks to them shall die."

The Merry Wives of Windsor, *Act V, Scene V,*
William Shakespeare, 1602

Chapter 14
A Light in the Dark

"Aveline? Can you hear me?"

It was Harold. He sounded close. About to answer back, Aveline remembered her earlier experience with the creepy puppet show. Was this another trick?

"Aveline?" This voice was Sammy's.

Aveline hesitated. They sounded real and they sounded scared. Pulling herself together, she called nervously in their direction.

"It's me, I'm over here."

More footsteps, sounding reassuringly heavy and solid. Then Harold and Sammy loomed into view, their faces shiny with either sweat – or fear.

"Aveline! What happened to you?" Harold said.

Aveline took a backward step, not yet sure if she could trust what she was seeing. Yes, they looked real enough, but so had the puppets at first. And nothing was ever what it seemed in this place. Noticing her nervousness, Harold held out his hands.

"It's okay, it's me. I mean…it's us – me and Sammy."

Sammy stepped forward and held up his phone.

"Look, Aveline, I'll prove it."

He held out the camera and beckoned Harold towards him. They put their arms around each other and posed for a selfie as if they were out for a Saturday afternoon and not hopelessly lost in an ancient burial chamber that was haunted by evil faeries. Sammy swiped his phone a couple of times and held it out for Aveline.

"See?" he said. "The camera never lies."

Aveline checked it. The boys looked like dark shadows, but she could just about see them both and neither had an elongated nose or twiggy fingers or cobweb strings sticking out of their back.

"Are you okay?" Harold said quietly. "I was on my own for a while, then I found Sammy."

Aveline explained what had happened to her, about finding herself alone and then being tricked by the puppet show.

"A puppet show," Harold said with a disgusted frown. "That's just...ridiculous."

"It was pretty creepy watching you and Sammy bounce around," Aveline admitted.

"Well, it's good to see you," said Harold, before furrowing his brow. "Hang on, how do we know *you're* real?"

Aveline reached out and squashed Harold's nose with the tip of her finger. "That real enough for you?"

"Now we've passed the scientifically proven finger-on-nose test –" Sammy said, making a rare joke – "what do we do now?"

Aveline told them what she'd decided. "You two have to go and find a way out," she said. "I don't know how, but you have to keep looking. I'm going to go find my uncle and then we'll come after you, but I don't want you taking any more risks on my behalf. My mum and aunt will be out of their minds. Your parents, too, Sammy. Someone has to try and let people know what's happened, and that *someone* is you two."

Harold frowned and looked at Sammy, who frowned back.

"What?" Harold said. "You think after all this we're going to leave you on your own?"

"I don't think that's a good idea, Aveline," Sammy said. "We don't even know which way is up and which is down, so I don't know what makes you think we're going to find a way out. Surely we're better off sticking together?"

"But I won't be on my own," Aveline said. "I'll be with my uncle. But while I'm looking for him, I won't have a chance to search for an escape route, that's why you have to do it. I mean – we must know something about this place that might give us a clue?"

"We know it's old," Harold said. "And they used to bury people here."

"And we know the entrance is blocked," Sammy said, miserably. "I've walked around the outside of this place about a hundred times, and I can't remember seeing anything else that looked like a way in."

But what the boys said had triggered something in Aveline's mind. It was as if they'd set off a chain reaction in her memories. Gears clicked into place. Images flashed across her mind like she was searching through the internet. Names and places. Books and objects. She remembered being back in her uncle's study, staring up at his wall. The photograph of the excavation. The marker on the map.

That was it.

They hadn't known what a long barrow was, so they'd looked online.

"Harold," Aveline said, trying to dampen the excitement that rippled through her body. "That thing we read, online, do you remember? It said something about this place and the midwinter solstice sunrise."

Harold frowned.

A moment later, his eyes widened.

"The sunrise! It said that once a year, the rising sun illuminates *the passage* and *the chamber*."

"The solstice," Sammy said. "That's today. At least I think it is? But I have no idea what time the sun rises. None of our phones are working correctly. Maybe we've missed it? It's hard to tell just how long we've been in here."

"Well, assuming we haven't missed it," Aveline said. "I think this is our chance to get out. It's a once-a-year event and if we do miss it, then that's it. We're trapped like everyone else."

"What about the other special days, Aveline?" Harold asked. "You know, the days your uncle held the séances?"

"The thing we read didn't mention the sun shining in here at any other time. I think those days were good for contacting the dead, but I think in terms of escape, the midwinter solstice is our only chance."

Aveline noticed that Harold had become distracted while she was talking, and he was now gazing down the tunnel with a puzzled expression.

"What is it?" Sammy said. "Is someone coming?"

"No, it's fine," Harold said. "It's just...don't you think it's getting brighter in here?"

Harold was right. The thick gloom was melting away. The ever-present shadows shrank back as if scolded. The mists swirled uneasily.

"Is this it?" Aveline whispered. "Is the sun rising?"

"If it is the sunrise, then we need to follow where it leads," Sammy said. "Aveline is right. It's a once-a-year event. Our one chance to find a way out. And it's not going to last long."

"Well, what are we waiting for?" Harold cried. "Let's go."

Aveline could feel the energy radiating off Harold and Sammy as they turned, waiting for her to follow. Yet inside Aveline a battle raged. On one side, there was cold, tired Aveline, who wanted to get out of the barrow more than anything she'd ever wanted before. The Aveline who was desperate to see her mum and aunt and reassure them that she was safe. The Aveline that wanted to follow the boys like an eager puppy chasing a ball, because it meant rescue and warmth and freedom.

And yet…

On the other side, there was Little Ave, Uncle Rowan's niece. The girl who'd been desperate to solve the riddle of his disappearance. The girl who had wanted to cry when she saw how broken and bewildered he was. This was the Aveline that wasn't prepared to accept that Lord Hemlock had taken someone she loved or that there was nothing she could do about it.

On and on this battle raged, until bloodied and bruised, a victor emerged.

She'd made her decision. She had to stick with it.

"You go," Aveline said. "Like we agreed. Follow the light, see where it leads. Try and get out. I can't just walk out and abandon my Uncle Rowan. Not now I know he's in here."

"But, Aveline," Harold pleaded, "You said yourself: we have one chance."

She could see Harold's exhausted expression, as if he'd just won the lottery but lost the ticket.

"It's alright," Aveline said. "Trust me, I'm going to find him. You and Sammy need to go now. Tell my mum and aunt that I'm okay and then get home safely."

"*How* will you find him?" Sammy said. "He could be anywhere, you could be looking for years!"

"I can sense him, like I did before. When I really concentrate, it's like there's this bond between us, a string that ties us together. All I need to do is follow it."

"You're not joking, are you?" Harold said.

"No, he's counting on me. You have to go and find the way, tell everyone what's happened. I'll be right behind you, I promise."

"I don't like this," Harold said. "Not one little bit. We always stick together. Whatever happens."

"Can't say I feel good about it either," Sammy said. "Leaving you alone in here doesn't feel right."

"I'm not going to argue," Aveline insisted. "There isn't time. The solstice only comes once a year so the best way you can help me is by following the light and finding your way out. Otherwise, nobody will know what happened to us." She glanced at Sammy and smiled. "Also, we need Sammy to be a famous paranormal expert, one day, so we can go around to his mansion and swim in his pool. Now go!"

Aveline gave them both a hard shove, then turned and started running back in the direction they'd come before her nerve gave out. She only glanced back once. The light grew weaker the farther away she got. It didn't feel good to be running back into the darkness. Pausing, she caught her breath and gathered herself, trying to dampen the flicker of panic that smouldered deep down inside. It was the first time they'd seen a glimpse of hope and now her mind was telling her what a fool she'd been. Turning down the chance of escape? It was hard to believe she'd actually done it. She wanted to give herself a hard kick on the shins for being so daft. But she'd made her decision, and despite her fear and misgivings, she knew it was the right one. She wasn't about to give up on her uncle. And if she was quick, this could all be over soon.

Calming herself, she pulled out her old photograph of them by the lake and focused on it. Then she closed her eyes and whispered under her breath.

"Uncle Rowan, it's me, Aveline. It's time to go. Show me where you are."

As she opened her eyes, to her relief she felt her uncle's presence.

He was close.

Feeling her spirits lift, she imagined Harold and Sammy emerging outside, before running down the hill to get help. They would be waiting for her, no doubt about that. Waiting for them both – her *and* Uncle Rowan. All she had to do was guide him out. She could be back with the boys in minutes.

As she walked down the tunnel, it reminded her of looking for something hidden, and having someone alongside you saying *warm, warm, you're getting warmer*. Someone, somehow, was guiding her. Then, before she knew it, Aveline was standing outside another door.

She'd found him.

She was about to open it when she heard the tap-tap-tap of footsteps behind her. Whirling around, she saw a faint light. Not the strong sunlight she'd just left behind, but the weak glow of a phone.

"We couldn't do it, Aveline. Sorry!"

"Oh no," Aveline gasped. "Harold!"

"Yep, you can't get rid of us that easily," Sammy said, grinning over Harold's shoulder.

"And no need to squash my nose again, it really is us. Harold and Sammy. In the flesh."

"What are you doing?" Aveline said, trying to sound angry when she actually felt like her birthday had come early. "I thought we'd agreed you were going to go ahead and find the way out?"

"We did agree," Harold said. "Then Sammy and I

changed our minds. We were in this together from the start and we'll be in this together until the end. Just let's hurry, please."

"Sunrises don't last long," Sammy said. "We might only have a few minutes left for all we know. Then we're here for another year and personally, I think that means we'll end up lost in here for ever like everyone else that's been snatched."

"Well, let's go save my uncle then," Aveline said, turning her attention back to the door and pushing it open.

They were back in the study. Uncle Rowan was sitting at his desk.

Only this time, there was someone sitting beside him.

A girl, with messy hair and glasses.

"They commonly report, that all uncouth,
unknown Wights are terrifyed by nothing earthly
so much as by cold Iron."

The Secret Commonwealth,
Robert Kirk, 1691

Chapter 15

A Trick Up the Sleeve

Aveline's mouth dropped open as she stared at her mirror self.

It was her, only she looked young yet at the same time aged; skin grey and crinkled, hair hanging down like damp straw.

"That's…" Harold didn't finish his sentence. They could see for themselves.

The Aveline sitting at the desk had her arm around Uncle Rowan and smiled at them triumphantly. Behind the glasses, her eyes were dark and cold and dead. Her clothes were the same as Aveline's, except they were dirty and ragged. The coat was missing a sleeve. The jeans were ripped and torn. And her feet were bare and blackened, with long toes that ended in knife-like nails.

"Uncle Rowan?" Aveline said.

"He's busy and can't be disturbed," the other Aveline snapped back, the voice a cold and brittle imitation.

"Yes," mumbled Uncle Rowan. "I'm busy as a bee, very busy."

"Yes, he has lots of lots of work to do, so go away."

Aveline paused. She suddenly remembered something. Something she was desperately hoping that Harold had remembered, too.

Because if he had, then it changed *everything*.

"We want to make a deal," Aveline said. "Don't you want to know what it is?"

The other Aveline's lip curled up and her eyes narrowed suspiciously.

"What could you possibly have that I could want?"

"Well, it's funny," Aveline said. "But we have this really weird thing that we found, it's like a clasp, got a skull on it, with little wings. Funnily enough, we saw it on a portrait in here. Belongs to someone called Lord Hemlock, do you know him?" She turned to Harold. "Harold, do you remember that thing I gave you and told you to put in your pocket?"

Harold looked utterly confused.

230

"The thing we found in my uncle's desk. It had been buried in the ground." Aveline lowered her voice to a whisper. "The thing *they* don't like!"

Comprehension dawned on Harold's face. Hurriedly, he reached into his jeans pocket, his fingers frantically searching. Aveline was just beginning to get worried when she saw him smile.

"Ah, yes, here we go," he said. "Turns out I did remember to bring it after all."

Aveline held out her hand to him and Harold placed something in it.

Something cold and hard and pointy.

"Let me see," the other Aveline said, rising menacingly to her feet, long toenails click-clacking on the floor.

"You can have it if you let my uncle come with us."

The other Aveline's eyes narrowed suspiciously, before she grinned, revealing teeth that looked like tiny black daggers.

"Suit yourself," the other Aveline said. "There's no escape, I'm afraid, so feel free to take him along with you on your endless wanders. I'll have fun watching you all stumble along in the dark. So, now we've settled that matter, give me the clasp, now, or I'll cut it out of your hand myself."

"Aveline." Uncle Rowan stood up from his chair.

"Yes?" Aveline and the other Aveline said in unison.

Uncle Rowan looked between the two of them.

"Why do you both look the same?" he asked.

"Because, Uncle Rowan, one's pretending to be me," Aveline said, suppressing a smile as she slid the iron nail Harold had passed her from her palm into the tips of her fingers. "I'm Aveline. I'm your niece. I'm Susan's daughter. We're your family. We're alive and well, and we love you and want you to come home."

The other Aveline raised a grubby hand to her mouth and giggled, black eyes widening in glee.

"What a lovely speech," she cackled. "Anyway, back to business. The clasp, if you please?"

"Aveline," Uncle Rowan warned. "Be careful, it's—"

"It's okay, uncle," she said, stretching out her hand. She held Uncle Rowan's gaze for a moment and smiled. "Trust me."

As the other Aveline stepped menacingly towards her, Aveline wrapped her right hand tightly around the old coffin nail. Now she just had to hope that the myths were true. She waited, holding her nerve as the other Aveline's clawed hand closed around hers.

At that moment, Aveline struck.

Grabbing the other Aveline's wrist, she drew out the nail and quickly pressed the point down into the back of her impersonator's hand and held it firm.

The other Aveline recoiled, her dark eyes scrunched in pain.

"Ow, that burns! It's iron! It's not allowed in here!"

Which only made Aveline press the point of the nail harder, feeling something soft and squishy move beneath it, as if the faery's hand was made of pretend skin and bones.

"Take it away!" the faery screamed. "It's forbidden!"

"It's working!" Harold cried. "Keep going!"

The faery's hand was like a fish, twisting and slippery, but Aveline held on tightly and pressed just a little harder.

"It's not nice being tricked, is it?" she yelled.

For one horrible moment, the faery's hand nearly wriggled free, but she redoubled her efforts and slowly, but surely, Aveline saw her mirror self begin to change. Its skin sagged and darkened, taking on the appearance of aged leather. The dead eyes rolled up until only the whites could be seen. Its twiggy limbs shrank and shrivelled. Finally, its hand slipped from hers. As it did, she heard a rattling whisper.

"You know, I never forget a face."

A second later, the other Aveline was gone. Something black and crooked flew across the wall and out of the door. Like a snake shedding its skin, empty clothes dropped to the floor. Spectacles clattered across the study floor and when Aveline picked them up, she saw that they weren't glasses at all, just a couple of spiky hawthorn twigs crudely twisted together.

The air seemed lighter. The shadows shrank back. The sense of menace that had stalked them through the darkness slowly receded.

"Looks like there's only one Aveline again," Harold said, clapping his hand on her shoulder. "That's a relief. Not sure I could handle having your evil twin hanging around, too."

"You didn't tell me you had a piece of iron!" Sammy said. "Why does it feel like you're always one step ahead of everyone?"

"Oh, you know – got to keep a few tricks up your sleeve," Aveline said with a smile. "Can't believe it actually worked though."

"It not only worked," Sammy said with an impressed nod. "You're now possibly the only person in the country to have defeated an evil faery – props!"

"You did it, Aveline," Harold said. "But we're not out

of the woods yet. We've got one chance to get out of here and we're running out of time."

"Okay," Aveline said. "Come on, Uncle, let's go!"

Uncle Rowan sat back down again and folded his arms.

"But…how do I know I can trust you?" he said. "I've been fooled so…so many times."

Crouching at his feet, Aveline took his hand. It quivered ever so slightly. She understood how he felt. She'd only been in here for a short while but had already developed a few trust issues of her own.

"Because it's me. I'm real. I'm alive. Can't you feel it?" she said, giving his hand a squeeze.

"I…think so," Uncle Rowan said. "But maybe it's better if I stay, just to be on the safe side?"

"Aveline," Harold pressed. "Come on, we need to leave."

Sighing, Aveline released her uncle's hand. Holding up the iron nail, she let him see it. His eyes narrowed.

"See this?" Aveline said. "It saved us. It's part of a collection that belongs to a brilliant archaeologist that I know. His name is Rowan Jones. He's amazing at what he does. Lots of people love him. He's kind and gentle. Really smart. And he's been missing for far too long. That's you, Uncle, and it's time you came back."

Eyes shining, Uncle Rowan reached out hesitantly towards the nail, stopping just short of touching it.

"I remember this," he said. "I found it on a dig. In Oxfordshire. I remember!"

With tears in his eyes, he reached towards Aveline and squeezed the tops of her arms. "Oh, Ave, can we go home now? I've had enough of this place."

"Yes, Uncle," Aveline said. "We can go right now."

"Come on, hurry, the sun's rising!" Harold urged again.

Aveline had to help her uncle out of his chair. His skin felt like paper and his legs were bowed and wobbly. Pulling off her woolly hat, she pulled it down over her uncle's head until it covered his ears. Then, leaning into him, she wrapped her arm around his waist. Harold stepped in on the other side and together they guided her uncle to the door. Her uncle's frailty made progress slow, but they got themselves back into the tunnel and began walking.

"Where's the light?' Sammy said in a panicked voice. "I can't see it."

"Just keep going," Aveline said. "It'll be there."

"We might have missed it for all we know," Harold said.

But they pressed on. Uncle Rowan mumbled to himself as they walked, but the rest of them were silent, their eyes roaming the darkness for any chink of light. Aveline listened to the slap of their footsteps, the murmurings of her uncle, and the weary breathing of her friends. It felt like she'd been on an endless journey and even now, she wondered if they would ever escape.

Up ahead, Sammy stopped.

"There!" Sammy cried. "Quick, I see it!"

Peering over his shoulder, Aveline saw it, too, a warm pool of light that made her want to cry out in relief. It was spreading across the tunnel floor, growing larger and brighter, as if a river made of fire was snaking down the passageway towards them. She wanted to run. They might have only seconds to spare for all she knew. Yet her uncle was still struggling to put one foot in front of another and so she called out to Sammy.

"Go, Sammy!"

This time he didn't need any encouragement and sprinted ahead.

The light grew brighter, so much so they had to squint. They could feel the sun's warmth on their skin. Shadows leaped back as if scalded by the light as the passageway illuminated with a fiery glow. It was a breathtaking sight as if they were seeing the sun in all its glory for the very first time.

Now, as well as the sunlight trail, they had Sammy's voice to guide them.

"That's it, nearly there!" he called back down the tunnel. "Come on, Uncle Rowan, Aveline and Harold have got you, you're nearly out!"

As they caught up, gasping for breath, Aveline saw Sammy silhouetted in front of a ball of fire, that rose between two huge stone slabs.

"That's it, that's the doorway," she whispered. "It's open!"

Sammy pushed on, calling to them, "Quickly!" before dropping to his hands and knees.

With panic setting in, Aveline and Harold guided Uncle Rowan to the doorway, seeing that it narrowed to a gap that was too small to walk through, but it certainly looked big enough to crawl through. They helped Uncle Rowan down onto his knees and pushed him forward.

"Keep going, Uncle, don't stop!"

Harold gestured to Aveline.

"After you," he said. "Don't worry, I'll be so close behind, you'll feel my breath on your ankles."

"That's something to look forward to." Aveline grinned before dropping to all fours and crawling into the narrow opening. Gravel ground into her palms and knees but she kept on going as if she was in a race. She could see Uncle

Rowan in front of her and something else; an eerie reddish glow, that grew steadily brighter. Cold air fanned her face. She heard the wind, brushing its way through the treetops. Gravel turned to grass, the snowy, frozen blades on her chin feeling like a kiss. She was outside, in the cold, beautiful air. In front of her, Uncle Rowan clambered stiffly to his feet. Aveline pulled herself out the last few metres and glanced back. She couldn't see Harold's face, but she could see his fringe, dangling in front of him like a millipede. Aveline helped him out, then they clambered to their feet and breathed the biggest sigh of relief.

As Harold dusted himself down, they heard a grating sound behind them as the sun's rays climbed away from the doorway. Then a solid *clunk* as if two heavy stone slabs had slammed together.

The grass sparkled as if someone had thrown a fistful of crushed ice across it. Sammy was beaming at her, the sunlight making his face shine, too. Behind her, Harold placed his hands on her shoulders before breaking into a dance and chanting deliriously:

"We did it, we did it!"

His joy was infectious and soon the three of them held hands and danced around Uncle Rowan, whose eyes were already growing clearer. A huge smile spread across his face and soon he was dancing with them. Aveline glanced around. There wasn't much sign that a festival had taken place there. Only a few crude bundles of straw tied in bunches and scraps of what might have once been clothes lay on the ground; remnants of what might have been pretend people brought alive by some dark faery magic.

Or might not have been.

"Let's get out of here," Aveline said, shivering. "Right now, I need to be as far away from *the barrow* as possible."

They walked along the edge of the wood until they reached the stile. Aveline prepared to help her uncle over, but to her surprise he clambered over with relative ease. Frowning, she peered at him.

"Uncle Rowan, are you feeling better?"

Grinning, he shrugged his shoulders.

"The only thing I know is that every step further away from that place I go, the lighter I feel. I can't believe you came and actually found me!"

"I'm so glad we did, Uncle, but let's keep moving."

In the distance, they heard people shouting to one another. Figures moved through the early morning rays. A dog barked. The next thing they saw was a group of police officers. Behind them were Aveline's mum and aunt, their eyes wide with both shock and relief.

"Faeries, come take me out of this dull world,
    For I would ride with you upon the wind,
        Run on the top of the dishevelled tide,
    And dance upon the mountains like a flame."

The Land of Heart's Desire,
William Butler Yeats, 1894

Chapter 16
Fond Farewells

Harold and Aveline stared intently at Sammy's phone. The three of them were huddled together on Aveline's bed at Uncle Rowan's house.

"Okay, ready?" Sammy asked.

They nodded eagerly.

"Here we go then," he said, adjusting his blue glasses and bending closer to the phone screen. "Possibly the first ever genuine photograph of a faery."

Grinning, Sammy opened his camera app and began swiping through the pictures. He paused at one. Expanded it. Moved on to the next one, and the one after that, doing the same thing with every one until a picture of him appeared, frowning into the camera. The photographs

243

he'd taken in the barrow were gone, each one now just a black screen.

"Sorry, Sammy, not sure what's happened there," Harold said. "But I don't think a bad selfie is going to make you famous."

Sammy scrolled through them again.

"I can't believe it, they were fine in the barrow! Where've they gone?"

"Who knows?" Aveline said. "Perhaps once you leave, they disappear? Faery magic or something. There's a lot of things about that place we'll never understand."

Sighing, Sammy clicked off his phone.

"I'm still going to write about it on the blog. I don't care if nobody believes me. I mean, it doesn't get many visitors anyway, but there are a few regulars who leave comments and stuff – I'm sure they'll appreciate it."

"You can count on two more visitors from now on," Harold said. "You could add some recipes on there, too, you know, show people what to do if they happen to have a spare bag of salt lying around."

Sammy gave him a brief smile, before glancing out of the window, his eyes ever watchful.

"Do you think you'll go back up there?" Aveline asked him. "You know, to the long barrow?"

"Yes," Sammy said. "In fact, we're all going back there with your uncle after lunch. He's got something he needs to return."

Aveline and Harold knew Sammy was right, but still, they hadn't been sure whether he was joking at first. But it appeared not, because an hour later they were trudging back up in the snow along with Uncle Rowan, who carried a small locked box in one hand.

"I remember when I first found it," he told them as they huffed and puffed up the hill. "I located the old excavations they did here. They were pretty much intact. Then I started coming up more often, and I eventually stumbled upon this strange clasp. It was unlike anything I'd ever seen in my archaeological career and, believe me, I've found some pretty strange things. It had this menace to it, as if it was alive or something. I knew it wasn't of human origin and it confirmed everything I had suspected about this place. I knew I shouldn't take it, but I did anyway. I couldn't resist. I took it home and locked it away, then the next day I came again and it was the solstice. I began to get this uncanny sense that I was being watched, only, every time I looked, I couldn't see anything. Then, as I was digging, I heard voices calling for help, and I saw a light in the darkness, like a lantern.

I followed it and the next thing I knew, I was stumbling around in the dark with no idea what had happened."

"We know how that feels," Harold said, his cheeks red with all the exertion. "Something very similar happened to us."

They arrived at the barrow and caught their breath. In the grey stillness of a winter day, it had lost some of its awe-inspiring power. However Aveline couldn't help shivering, the memories of what lay within all too fresh. Uncle Rowan opened his lockbox and held the clasp in his palm for a moment.

"I should have left it where I found it," he said almost to himself. "At the time, I had every intention of sending it on to a museum to see what they made of it. But I think in this case, it's best returned to its owner. You never know what he might do in order to get it back."

He then walked towards the entranceway and knelt down, his fingers scrabbling in the dirt and gravel.

As Aveline and the others watched, a silhouette appeared on top of the barrow. Crooked and gaunt, with the sinking sun at its back, it stood silent and unmoving. A chill breeze blew across the field, making Aveline shiver despite her winter layers. She couldn't be sure, but she thought she could hear her name being called on the wind.

Aveline…Aveline…

"Is that…?"

As Harold trailed off, a low, sinister chuckle echoed over the fields.

"Um…Uncle Rowan," Aveline called. "Hurry, we should go now, I mean, right now!"

"Coming!" he called.

From far off, a church bell rang. And as Aveline, Harold and Sammy watched, the silhouette appeared to melt into the gloom of the winter afternoon.

"It's back where it belongs," Uncle Rowan said when he returned, a little breathless from his digging.

"Okay, let's go," Aveline said, her eyes darting nervously over her uncle's shoulder.

"What's happened?" her uncle replied. "You all look a little nervous."

"Oh, you know, I just hope that's the last we've seen of Lord Hemlock."

"You think?" her uncle said. "You know, I really must do some more research on faeries."

"Sammy's a good place to start," Harold said. "He's an expert on these things."

Uncle Rowan put an arm around Sammy's shoulders.

"Well, you must tell me everything you know on the way home," he said. "Might stop me making any more silly mistakes in the future."

Aveline noticed Sammy smile. And did he puff his chest out just a little? Possibly. She knew that she, Sammy and Harold were going to be good friends, and the thought made her happy. She felt even happier once they'd left the long barrow way behind them.

They would be leaving Scarbury later that day. Aveline had invited Sammy to come and stay at her house in

Bristol after Christmas, since it wasn't far. Sammy had agreed, on the condition that Aveline help him write some articles for his blog. Not only had she been flattered, but she'd agreed immediately. It sounded right up her street. Besides, they had a bond now. An experience they wouldn't – and couldn't – forget.

"Looks like it might snow again soon," Sammy said, glancing at the sky.

"We best text ahead for some more hot chocolate then," Harold said.

"I'll make it when we get back," Uncle Rowan said. "I have a lot of making up to do with Susan and Lilian, so a mug of something extra sweet might help."

He'd come back from the police station earlier that day, having been asked to go in and attend an interview. From what she could understand, he'd told the police that he'd hit his head near the barrow many years ago and had suffered amnesia. This had led to him leaving the area and not knowing who he was, until the day he'd found his way back to the barrow and his memory had come flooding back.

It was a decent enough story, Aveline thought, and not *too far* from the truth. The children had told the police that they'd become lost and disorientated in the snow.

Which again, wasn't too far from the truth. Luckily, the police seemed more concerned about them being safe rather than worrying about the exact details of what had happened, which seemed to suit everyone involved. Aveline wondered what Uncle Rowan had told her mum and aunt. She had no idea where to begin. But she couldn't stop smiling when she remembered the look on her mum and aunt's face when they'd seen her walking down the hill from the long barrow with Uncle Rowan in tow.

Back in Uncle Rowan's kitchen, Aveline's mum and aunt looked as if they'd just returned from holiday. Their pale, tense expressions had been replaced by bright eyes and warm smiles. After Uncle Rowan served everyone up with a very generous helping of hot chocolate, they all sat and chatted. The house felt cheery and welcoming, as if it had forgotten it was supposed to be gloomy and empty.

"Well, we had a *very* interesting chat with Rowan earlier," Aunt Lilian said. "One day I hope to hear your version, Aveline. But I know that Susan, Rowan and I have *a lot* to thank you all for."

"So drink up and you can have a second helping," Aveline's mum said. "And after that, you can have a third if you like. I think you all deserve to be thoroughly spoilt for a day or two."

"Just a day or two?" Aveline said. "I would have thought a year or two, what do you think, Harold?"

"Oh, I totally agree," Harold said. "A rescue like this will need a very, very long time and a lot of sweet treats before we're all square. Sammy?"

"Definitely!"

Aveline had been bracing herself for more questions about their experience in the barrow, but it seemed everybody preferred talking about lighter subjects for the time being. She was sure that would come later, probably once she and her mum were alone.

They all walked Sammy back home later in the afternoon. His parents – after they'd calmed down – had allowed him to spend the rest of the morning with them. Uncle Rowan shook hands with Sammy for so long on his doorstep that Aunt Lilian had to order him to stop. When they got back, Aveline's mum told her to gather her stuff together. They would leave the house on the market, she said. Rowan had decided that living in Scarbury had lost a little of its appeal.

"But what will he do until then?" Aveline asked her mum. "We can't leave him here on his own."

"No, of course not," her mum said. "I've decided to keep him very close to us from now on. That's why we'll be having an extra guest."

That left Aveline feeling like Christmas Day had come early.

They texted Sammy again before they left and said they'd see him soon. He replied in his typical manner.

Stay safe. We all know what's out there.

See you soon ☺

Though Aveline did notice the addition of a smiley face.

Aunt Lilian organized a taxi to take them to the station. Harold's parents were coming up to Bristol and would be waiting to collect him.

"Okay, what have you got lined up next for us?" Harold said, as the train clickety-clacked its way along the tracks. "A weekend at an abandoned fairground? Maybe a short break at a haunted castle on the moors somewhere?"

Aveline adopted her most serious expression, which she'd learned from Sammy.

"Let's just wait and see, shall we?"

The End

*Prepare for the Scares and
Collect every Aveline Jones adventure*

Aveline Jones loves reading ghost stories, so a dreary half-term becomes much more exciting when she discovers a spooky old book. Not only are the stories spine-tingling, but it once belonged to Primrose Penberthy, who vanished mysteriously, never to be seen again. Intrigued, Aveline decides to investigate Primrose's disappearance.

Now someone... or something, is stirring. And it is looking for Aveline.

"Captivating and gorgeously written. I was definitely bewitched!" Michelle Harrison

The Bewitching of
AVELINE JONES
Phil Hickes

Aveline is thrilled when she discovers that the holiday cottage her mum has rented for the summer is beside a stone circle. Thousands of years old, the local villagers refer to the ancient structure as the Witch Stones, and Aveline cannot wait to learn more about them.

Then Aveline meets Hazel. Impossibly cool, mysterious yet friendly, Aveline soon falls under Hazel's spell. In fact, Hazel is quite unlike anyone Aveline has ever met before, but she can't work out why.

Will Aveline discover the truth about Hazel, before it's too late?

Look out for another spine-tingling series
from Phil Hickes

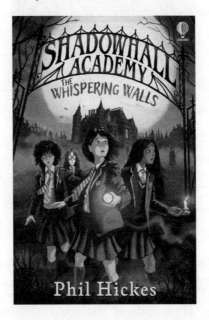

Welcome to Shadowhall Academy,
where spirits haunt the school halls…

"Genuinely chilling… Kids are going to absolutely
love it." Jennifer Killick, author of *Dread Wood*

"Boarding school and spookiness – Malory Towers
gone rogue!" Lesley Parr, author of
When the War Came Home